The Reaper Incarnate

A REAPED NOVELLA

Copyright

Dedication

This one is for Sammi and Lisa.
Thanks for creating the perfect opportunity for the
best tasting Peanut Butter and Jelly sandwich.

Prologue

"That's right baby," he moans as he shoves my head onto his miniscule dick. "Take all of it." Not a difficult task if I'm being honest.

"I want to go home and fuck my wife knowing your mouth was just there." He sounds like a fucking idiot and I bet his wife thinks so, too.

I release his needle dick with a pop and raise my head to look him in the face.

"Or you can go home and rape your step-daughter again?"

His eyes widen and his mouth drops in shock. He begins to push my head away as he stutters, but it's hard to move in a small Honda Fit.

"Who are you?" He chokes out when I sit back in the passenger seat.

"I'll give you three guesses." I smile wide, showcasing my bright white teeth.

"I don't know…" He shakes his head.

"You lose." I sing-song.

I pull the gun from my purse at my feet and press it to his forehead.

"No, wait…" I watch as his small flaccid dick spouts with piss.

"Gross." I screw up my face and pull the trigger.

The back of his head explodes all over the driver's side window and I feel blood splatter across my face. I smear my fingers through it and suck them into my mouth, nothing tastes better than the blood of a predator.

I reach behind his concave head and press my finger into the blood and brain matter mixture on the window.

Reaped.

Chapter One

Selene

The overhead streetlight casts a dim yellow aura around me as I lean against the pole waiting for him. I've tracked him for the past two weeks and the bastard has become predictable.

I'm standing outside of his favorite tavern - he hits this one up on Mondays and Fridays - and he'll stagger out in about ten minutes, looking for a taxi. I settled on this place for our *meeting* because the alleyway beside it is perfect for a clandestine hook up.

"See you next week, Charles." His voice grates on my nerves and when he laughs, I fantasize about cutting it out of his throat.

He stands beside me and peers up then down the street, looking for the bright yellow paint of a cab. I can feel the moment his eyes land on me because my skin crawls and I feel an uncontrollable urge to pop them out of his head.

"Have you been waiting long?" He slurs and I curl my hands into fists.

"About ten minutes." I keep my voice level and sweet.

I swing my gaze to meet his and feel the bile creep up my throat at his appreciative perusal. His highlighted blonde hair sways in the breeze and his green eyes crinkle with mirth. Those full lips pull up into a handsome smirk. He kind of looks like a Ken doll.

"I haven't seen you here before." He stumbles then rights himself.

"I've seen you." I say seductively and slowly flutter my lashes.

"Is that so?" He two-steps excitedly.

"Oh yes," I nod. "I think you are one of the most handsome men I've ever seen."

"No!" He pffts with his mouth and waves me off.

"Mmhmm." I nod again.

"Well, I'm here now." He holds his hands out and stumbles. "Question is, what are you going to do with me?"

See? Predictable cunt.

"Hmm." I tap my chin, pretending to be deep in thought. "How about we go down that pathway and get acquainted?"

"The alley?" His eyes widen with excitement.

"Why not?" I shrug.

He motions for me to lead the way and I grin knowing I have him right where I want him. I step into the alley and the little light from the streetlamp completely dissipates. It's pitch black and I can smell urine, making me gag.

It takes him all of three steps before he has my face pressed against the brick. I roll my eyes and pretend to panic.

"Hey." I call out. "Take it easy."

"You're an easy little bitch." He growls and the stench of whiskey on his breath floods my nostrils. "I usually like them fighting."

"I know." I say as I rear my head back and crack him in the nose.

He falls back against the adjacent wall, clutching his nose, and roaring. I stalk towards him and kick him swiftly in the balls, grinning when he falls to his knees.

His nose is running with blood and dripping off his chin. His hands are cupping his sac as he sways and cries, and I bend at the waist to meet him eye to eye.

"You've been naughty." I wag my finger at him. "Very naughty."

He begins to moan and plead with me to leave him alone.

"Can't do that." I straighten, "remember all those campus girls that begged for the same thing? You didn't show them mercy."

"Who are you?" Spit flies from his mouth and blood runs between his teeth.

"You all ask the exact same questions and expect an answer." I tsk. "What does it matter? You'll be dead soon."

The fucker throws his head back and laughs at my revelation. "Dead?"

"Yeah." I pull the knife out of its holster on my hip and point it at his face.

The smile falls from his mouth and his eyes darken with anger. I watch as he lifts one of his hands toward me and I swing the blade, cutting across the flesh at his wrist. The blood spurts and rapidly flows from the open arteries, hitting the pavement in large splatters.

His other hand grabs his wrist and I laugh as the blood oozes out around his fingers. He looks up at me with shock lining his features and leans over to puke at my feet. Lovely.

I knee him in the forehead and he falls back against the wall, his arms flying to his sides. Like taking candy from a fucking baby.

I bend down and grab his uncut wrist, slowly running the knife's edge over the skin, watching as it splits apart. He moans and tries to sit up but I've given him a few good cracks on the head, not to mention how drunk he is.

The blood pools around his hand and his body begins to twitch as death enters his limbs. I pull my finger through the crimson fluid and draw a scythe into the ground. Then I rise, wipe the blood off the blade with his shirt, and tuck it back in the holster.

I leave the alley whistling softly and planning my next hit.

Chapter Two

Selene

The worst thing about my life revolving around my work is that I'm always fucking hungry. Whether it be my next victim, or food, it's all the same. I shut down the darknet chat on my laptop and try to calm myself. So many motherfuckers on there looking for women and children to abuse and they are all falling into my carefully placed traps.

I watch the world go by out the window of my small apartment, shoveling my burger into my mouth as if it's my last meal. Ketchup oozes out and drips onto my plate, and I absently swipe it up with my finger and suck it clean.

I close my eyes and smile at the memory of my last kill, his blood covered skin giving me the same feeling as a bright Christmas tree would for a child. I can't tell you how many people I've wiped from the face of the earth and getting vengeance for those who were victimized by worthless pieces of shit.

I am no fucking saint, but someone has to right the wrongs of those who have no remorse for their actions. Hell, I don't give a shit if they feel remorse or not, there is no forgiveness when it comes to the predators of this world. Nothing pisses me off more than a man who thinks he has the right to touch a woman or a child, just because they smile in their direction or give them a boner, just for looking good.

Everyone knows there's a vigilante running around town, slaying those who prey upon the innocent or vulnerable. I find my kills on the darknet, searching for the sick fucks who answer to my ads of wanting torture, and then let them lead me to all their friends. Obviously, no one knows it's me, because I don't want the praise or jail time that comes along with it.

I just want those to pay who can't keep their dicks and hands to themselves.

I've been posing as a prostitute for years now, and the amount of devils in disguise I've come across is disgusting. I always find the irony in using sex as a weapon to draw them in. Kind of feels like karma and a good way to get revenge.

I make them all suffer, but the ones I stalk who have put their vulgar dicks near a child? Well, I can be a little dramatic with their exits sometimes.

It can take weeks of learning their patterns, and I enjoy the hunt just as much as the kill.

My heart rate spikes with excitement at the thought of my next job. He is a typical rich asshole who thinks his shit doesn't stink, but he has so many skeletons in his closet and I know I'm going to love making him suffer in the worst way. He loves kids a little too much, and women are never the same after being with him. He is sadistic, and he gets off on their pain and tears.

I've been watching him for the last week or two, seeing the most fucked up deals take place, and I hunger to carve him to pieces with my knife. I can see his clean canvas in my mind, becoming mixed with blood and slashes as he cries for mercy. I can't wait to hear that sick fucker beg.

I'd bathe in his blood for those lost at his hands.

I finish my burger and drop the plate in the sink, wandering into my bedroom to find my notebook. I keep tabs on everyone I'm hunting, burning the papers when I'm done.

I glance over my notes, memorizing as much as I can. He meets with his friends every Wednesday at the bar on Main Street, usually trying to lure some poor woman into his grasp. He has lunch at the Chinese takeout downtown every Thursday and Friday, there he meets another person who just happens to be on my list, and this person is ironically the guy who's sold him children previously. The last kid was an eight-year-old boy.

I scowl and drop my notebook, running my fingers through my long blonde hair and pull sharply to feel the burn. I can't lose control of my emotions, no matter how angry my findings make me.

I should have a plan before spraying brain matter and blood everywhere. If I slash him to pieces too quickly, he won't suffer, and this man needs to suffer badly.

He has a son who I assume is as bad as he is, but I haven't set my eyes on him just yet.

Daddy dearest ought to go first, then his child trafficking friend is next. I'll get around to the rich asshole son after that.

I'd already put myself in the rich asshole senior's path, making sure he noticed me. I bumped into him as he was leaving the Chinese place the other day, pretending to apologize dramatically while reining in my need to gut him right there in the street.

I'm crazy, not stupid.

I made sure to wear the smallest amount of clothing possible, allowing him to steady me from the collision as his eyes took me in. He was interested, which made everything so much easier for the next time I confronted him. He was going to think he'd hit the fucking jackpot when I just happen to be at the Chinese place for lunch before he arrives, and I'll let him pay for my food because it's the least the asshole can do.

Men always think you owe them after they do something nice for you, because they're fucking pigs. They only hold the door open for you so they can check your ass out as you leave, and they can be so self-righteous that they think they're doing you a favor for letting you choke on their pathetic dicks as if it were a gift just for you.

He'll be the one choking when I cut his dick off and shove it down his throat for choking the last woman he had to death.

Chapter Three

Selene

"Order up for Selene!" The guy behind the counter yells. I head to the front of the restaurant and take the bag containing my chicken chow mein, smiling at the guy.

"Selene." I hear his voice and goosebumps break out along my skin. "That's a lovely name."

I look up into the piece of shit's nearly black eyes and put on my prettiest smile, "my mother named me after the Greek goddess of the Moon."

"Here you are Henry, same as always." He's handed his lunch.

"I will pay for Selene's today as well, Tyler." Henry says with a smile my way. Look at that, all these asshole predators are so fucking predictable.

"Oh no!" I throw my hand to my exposed cleavage, watching as his eyes follow. "You don't have to do that, Sir."

His eyes shine with appreciation at my calling him Sir and I feel the bile scorching up my fucking throat.

"It's the least I can do for nearly mowing you down last week," he winks.

I giggle, making sure my tits bounce, and watching as his eyes latch on to their movements. He hands a credit card to Tyler and leans his hip on the counter. He looks sharp for a man in his late fifties, a tailored suit, expensive leather shoes, and what looks to be an authentic gold tie clip.

His salt and pepper hair is combed back over his head to hide his balding crown and his face is clean shaven. He's handsome and to the unsuspecting woman, I would assume he's alluring, but to me he's a bag of shit and I can hardly stand the fucking stench.

"Are you bringing that back to your office to eat?" He asks as he takes the receipt and thanks Tyler.

"Oh, I don't have an office," I look up at him through my dramatic false lashes. "My job is a bit...well...unconventional."

We step out onto the street and he gives me a slow once over, his eyes devouring me from my feet up. He knows exactly what I mean by unconventional.

He reaches into his inside blazer pocket and hands me a business card. Henry Walton. C.C.R.E. Import and Export services.

"Call me to discuss business sometime." His fingers brush along my arm and I plaster a smile on my face. *Don't kill the cunt on the street*, I pray to myself.

"I will, Henry." I watch as he steps to a black Rolls Royce and gives me a final look over his shoulder.

Henry doesn't have a single fucking clue what he just got himself into.

I lift the hood of my ankle length black trench and stand across the street from Henry's mansion. Tonight, there's a drop off from the piece of shit human trafficker and I need to be here to watch as much as I can.

I hear heavy metal music blare as a sleek black Dodge Challenger comes veering from up the street. I hide further behind the large oak and watch as the wrought iron gates open. The car stops just inside and two guys step out. I can't really distinguish their features but they look like fucking thugs.

Both have black bandanas on their heads and dressed in big baggy jeans, with leather jackets covering their frames. They lean against the car and one sparks a joint, taking a deep toke before handing it to the other.

This is who Henry associates with? A bunch of fucking gang bangers? They are a direct contrast to the businessman image he is trying to portray and the only thing I can think of is that he hired some goons for the exchange that's about to go down.

They smoke their joint with minimal interaction and a few minutes later I see a large cargo van pull up to the gates. It's black with blacked out windows and the license plates are missing. Not fucking suspicious at all.

The gangsters straighten up when the van rolls through the gates and they follow behind it on foot, reaching for their pieces tucked into the backs of their jeans.

They get further away and out of my line of sight, and I huff against the tree in frustration. If I want to know more, I will have to get closer, and to get closer means I have to fuck the old man.

Guess it's time to set up a business meeting with the fucker.

I flip the thick, expensive looking business card between my fingers and sigh, it's so fucking hard keeping up with a charade, but I took on this line of work so I will see it to the end.

I dial the number for his cell phone and gag when he picks up.

"Walton here."

"Henry?" I make myself sound innocent and confused, "Sorry, may I speak with Henry?"

"Selene?" His voice lowers and I can hear the fucking undercurrents of satisfaction in it.

"Yes, it's me." I giggle.

"I'm happy you called. What can I do for you?" Why does he make that sound so fucking slimy?

"I... ah... wanted to discuss business?" I saturate my tone with uncertainty.

"You called the right place. Where shall we have this discussion?"

"I usually have them in my client's cars..."

"I'll meet you at the corner of Elmer and Delia." He cuts me off. "Same car as earlier."

Before I can even open my mouth to confirm, I hear the dial tone in my ear and growl at his confident manner. I can't wait to see him scared and begging me for mercy.

I make the choice to dress in my appropriate business attire and I straighten out my long wavy blonde hair, letting it hang loose down my back. I line my big baby blues in kohl, making them pop even more, and then I brush some blush onto my freckled cheeks, giving my pale skin some color.

I squeeze my girls into a leather crop top, grinning when their fullness nearly pops me in the chin, and then I pair it with a leather mini, the bottoms of my ass cheeks peeking out. My best fucking business suit.

I finish it off with a pair of thigh high heels because, duh, Pretty Woman, and pull my trench over the top. I give myself a once over in the mirror and chuckle at my appearance, thank God for the genes that make me look at least five years younger than my twenty-five. I know Mr. Walton likes them young.

I'm ready to get this shit started and I can feel my skin crawling with the need for blood.

Chapter Four

Selene

My heels click on the pavement as I make my way towards the Rolls Royce, the driver exits the vehicle to open the back door for me and gives us privacy.

I murmur a polite thank you as I ease myself inside, finding myself beside a beaming Henry Walton.

He wastes no time handing me a champagne glass, his fingers brushing against mine slightly.

"Selene, I'm so glad you called," he says with a toothy grin, eyeing my trench coat with annoyance.

I bite back a scoff and slip the apparent offending piece of clothing off my shoulders, pretending to admire the interior of the car.

"What a beautiful car you have. It's so roomy."

He licks his lips as his eyes roam my barely covered body, resting on my tits with no shame.

"I do enjoy beautiful things. Can we jump straight into business talk?" He asks, his voice sending unwanted shivers down my spine that he misreads as pleasure.

Typical sleazebag thinking he's making me cream in my panties with the temptation. My coochie is as dry as a nun's, thanks to him.

I bat my lashes at him and tuck a loose piece of my blonde hair behind my ear to act shy. Men like Henry feel powerful for dominating the quiet girls and turning them into freaks in the sheets.

"Of course, Mr. Walton. What would you like to know?"

He boldly places his hand on my thigh, his eyes darkening.

"How about you suck me off and we'll talk after that? Kind of like a try before you buy?" Is he for real?

I giggle, biting my lip as I peer over at him.

"Show me what goods I'm working with then, and I'll see if I can impress you," I say coyly, a deep chuckle coming from him as he reaches for his belt.

"Curious little thing, aren't you? How long have you been in the job? I haven't seen you before, and I think I'd remember a pretty face like yours."

He pulls his dick free and I lick my lips when I know he's watching. He's a decent size, but I bet he has no fucking idea how to use it. They rarely do, which is why they prey on those who are too innocent to know the difference. It gives them an ego boost to make someone cry.

"Oh wow, Mr. Walton, I don't think I'll be able to take it all. I'm still pretty new at this, so you might have to guide me," I gasp, putting a hand over my mouth for dramatics.

I know how to take dick, but it does wonders for his ego.

He smirks, encouraging me to slide closer to him.

"I'll show you just how I like it. So, this time is free?" He asks, waiting for me to get onto my knees on the seat and his eyes drift over me to stare at my ass in the air. I can't wait to bleed the dick-bag out.

I nod, trying to look nervous as I lean down, stretching my mouth to accommodate him. He lets me slide my mouth up and down his length a few times before his fingers thread through my silky straight hair, tightening to the point of pain as I expected he would.

"Open that pretty mouth all the way for me. Yes, that's it," he murmurs, before slamming my head down firmly, causing me to choke.

He keeps moving my head how he wants me, not giving a shit that I'm choking on saliva and his stupid dick.

"You like that, you little whore? You like choking on my fucking cock?" He growls, tightening his fist in my hair even more until he's relentlessly fucking himself with my face.

My eyes water, and my stomach lurches as he reaches past me and slaps my ass hard, showing me the monster he hides away, as he keeps speaking down to me like shit.

"I bet you've taken a lot of dicks, you filthy slut. You'd be nothing without men like me helping you pay your way in society. Do you think of all that cum you take whenever you pay a bill? When you eat your lunch? Girls like you need men like me, because it's the only way someone could ever want you."

I choke some more, his hand coming down hard on my ass again. I let him belittle me until he holds my face down and grunts his release.

He lets me choke on his dick and cum for a moment before removing his grip and allowing me to sit back. I wipe the moisture from under my eyes and catch my breath, running my tongue over my lips and giving him a sweet smile.

"Thank you, Mr. Walton," I force out, knowing it's the right thing to say as his eyes light up while he absently fixes his pants. He looks thoughtful for a moment before replying.

"I think this will be an exceptionally good investment. It's been a long time since I've come across a woman with manners and who acknowledges what I give her. I'm taking you to my house to clean up," then he grabs his phone and sends a text, the driver instantly climbing in behind the wheel.

This is not part of my plan, but I'm not going to say no to being invited into his house. I have to scope it out eventually, so it just makes my work a little easier without having to be so sneaky.

We don't speak the entire drive, but he won't shut the fuck up once when we arrive, enjoying showing off all his money and possessions. He takes my arm and guides me up the front steps, leading me into the main room that houses the most pompous works of art I've ever seen.

Most are paintings of himself, but there are a few of himself and whom I would assume is his son the further into the house we go. It just makes me want to kill him even more, no one should be that far up their own ass.

We walk through multiple rooms and hallways, and I try hard to remember as much as I can. I need to map the place out on paper when I get home so I can add to my plan of attack.

Once in the bathroom, he points to the sink and a small cupboard.

"Everything you need should be in there. I'll be in my office, one of the staff will show you where to go when you're done," then he turns and leaves me alone, like the stupid idiot that he is.

I quickly clean my face and rinse my mouth out with some mouthwash, glaring at the painting above the toilet of him naked. That's a little weird.

I take my time as I wander back through the house, adding to my mental map and wishing I had my knife on me to get it over with, but too many people know I'm with him, so I have no choice but to wait.

My heels seem to echo through the house on the marble floors, and I slow when I get to the kitchen, finding his son drinking a bottle of water, his throat working as he swallows. He's only in a pair of shorts, and my eyes linger on his tattoo covered abs before I look up at his face.

He works out, that's for sure.

He finally glances over at me, his eyes widening in surprise at the company before his nostrils flare and his eyes narrow.

"Who the fuck are you?" He growls, reminding me that this ab god is just a junior version of his asshole daddy. I can practically smell the money and arrogance on him.

I give him a bright smile, clasping my hands together in front of me and drawing his attention right to my tits as the leather pulls tighter across them, pushing them further together.

"I'm sorry, I'm a little lost. Do you know where Mr. Walton's office is? He told me to find him when I was finished in the bathroom," I ask softly, his gaze snapping back to mine. He takes me in for a second before rolling his eyes.

"Henry's office is back down the hallway and up the stairs. It's on the left." He grunts, turning and stalking out of the room.

"I'm Selene," I blurt out, making him pause in the doorway. He peers over his shoulder at me, pity underlining his features before he snaps out of it and snorts.

"Good for you, I don't give a fuck," then he leaves me standing there without a backwards glance.

His ass is alright, too.

I head back in the direction he told me to go, but someone steps in front of me and blocks my path.

"Mr. Walton had to take a business call and has asked me to show you out."

No apology, nothing. Typical rich asshole move.

I give him a smile and nod.

"I completely understand, I'd hate to be in his way. Please tell him thank you for the hospitality he gave me," I beam, wanting to puke at my own voice. I hate my job sometimes because I am not the type to be sweet, let alone grateful.

He nods, motioning behind me to get me to walk, making sure to stay by my side until we reach the door. I'm hoping he'll at least call me a cab, but the moment I am out the door, it's shut right behind me, and I'm on my own.

I roll my eyes and walk down the driveway, heading towards home.

His son's car speeds past me and I snort, not at all surprised that

Walton Junior doesn't offer me a ride.

Zander Walton is a daddy's boy, and I can't wait to get to work on him, too.

It's going to be such a shame to waste something that looks so good, I can't lie.

Chapter Five

Zander

My father and the dirty fucking prostitutes he brings to our house, I am about to fucking lose my shit. I pull the car out of the garage and speed down the driveway. It's not until I've hit the bottom that I see the girl walking alone. Should I wait here and pick her up?

Fuck it, she made her choice with him and now she can fucking walk in it.

I pull out onto the street and press the Bluetooth button on my wheel.

"Call Blaze."

"Calling Blaze." I've set my spoken voice to an Australian female who sounds as hot as fucking sin and I've named her Jocelyn.

"Sup?" Blaze's deep voice fills my Vette.

"We need to make a move on this bastard because I am fucking losing it." I snarl.

"Bro, hold it down. You need to breathe. It's coming and soon. Do not fuck our plans up or else I will kill you as well."

That was Blaze. We've been friends since middle school but the guy wouldn't bat an eye if he had to kill me.

"Yeah." I scrub a hand down my face and try to relax.

"Come over and do some lines." He says and hangs up.

I was doing good until he brought one into the house. Was it fucking necessary? Did it need to be so blatant in my face so soon after my mother's death?

I pull a U-turn, burning my tires, and head back towards Blaze's. I need a fucking night to relax and not think of all the shit that's weighing me the fuck down.

When I pull into his driveway, I can hear the music blaring and a line of other cars parked. Looks like a party, and I'm ready to lose myself in coke and pussy.

I walk into the house to see girls dancing on the tables with their tits out and random couples making out in darkened corners. Fuck yes.

"Zan!" I hear Blaze call out and I turn into the kitchen.

He has his table set up with a buffet of drug choices and a girl is kneeling in front of him sucking his dick, his piercing glinting in the kitchen lights.

"When you said a few lines, I thought you meant a few lines, not this shit." I grin and bump fists with him.

"Sit down, bro." He points to a bitch to the right, "fill Stacey's mouth with something."

"My name is Tracy." She rolls her eyes but comes forward anyways.

I pull out a chair and grin when she kneels in front of me and undoes my pants. Blaze has the best fucking parties.

"Take one." He says as he chucks me a bag of pills.

I open the bag and pop one in my mouth, swallowing it dry, and then I'm feeling lips wrap around my dick. This is what life is supposed to be like.

"All your dicks are being sucked and mine is lonely sitting on my balls."

I open my eyes at Santos' voice and grin when I see the bastard leaning against the fridge with a beer to his mouth. He's a crazy Mexican and loves to watch anything bleed. I really do mean anything.

Blaze groans and I look over at him with his head tipped back and his mouth open wide. He's a scary looking motherfucker with that angry scar down his face and standing close to six and a half feet. None of us get in his way because he's fucking mean and like I said before, he doesn't care who he has to kill.

This is just what I needed to get my mind off my father and the girl with the big blue eyes. Just thinking about her tits has me cumming down Stacey's throat.

"Yes, Stacey." I groan and she slaps my thigh.

"My name is fucking Tracy." She retorts as she wipes my cum from her lip.

What the fuck ever.

"Zan." Santos calls out. "Tuck your little white dick away and come check something out."

"Fuck you." I grin and get up from my seat.

Whatever pill Blaze gave me is working fast and the room begins to haze around the edges. I grab a beer from the fridge and follow Santos into the billiards room. There on one of the tables is a girl hogtied and Darius is plowing into her from behind.

"Holy fuck." I chuckle.

"She consented." Santos laughs and pulls out his switchblade. "I want to watch her bleed a bit, what do you think?"

He gets that wicked look in his eye and I know I'm in for a show.

I shrug and watch as he sets his beer down on the table and stands to the side of the chick. The noises she's making sounds like enjoyment, so I lean against the wall and take a swig of my beer.

Santos runs the blunt side of his blade along her back, underneath her hogtied limbs, and then runs it down between her ass cheeks. Santos has an unhealthy obsession with blood and he loves to see it run from his victims or his sexual partners, it makes no fucking difference.

Darius doesn't slow his thrusts, even though Santos' blade comes close to his dick.

"Look at her pussy, Zan." Santos says as the tip of the blade presses against her asshole. "Isn't she pink and pretty?"

Darius slams in one more time and groans his release, the girl shudders and her screams are muffled by the gag in her mouth. Darius pulls out and grabs Santos' beer, downing its contents in one fucking go.

"What's up Zan?" He grins as his fucking dick flops around, still wet from the girl's pussy.

"Nothin' man, looks like you guys got this party started early." I grin at him.

"That's sweet pussy." He thumbs over his shoulder.

I watch as Santos drops his pants and lines himself up to the girl's entrance, his knife resting on her lower back. He eases himself inside and scoops up his knife. I know what comes next and I'm not much of a fan. I push off the wall just as Santos' knife cuts into the girl's lower back and Darius is right back there, both dipping into her blood with their fingers as the girl screams.

Not my thing.

I leave the room and stumble towards the back porch, my vision blurring. This is the fucking life, not having to watch flesh exchanges and crying bitches in your own front yard, that shit isn't fun on any day.

Chapter Six

Selene

I finally get home and curse when I pull off my thigh highs, blisters raw on my feet. The fucking asshole. No Ubers were around that area and I just decided to fuck it and walk home. Worst mistake.

At least something good came from the fucking bullshit, I got a tour of the cunt's house, and now I have to make a complete plan. This isn't like any of my usual victims, Henry Walton is a big fucking fish and I can't trap him in a car to blow his brains out. It just won't work.

I have to plan this out to a T and also consider every fucking alternative that can happen. I'm also working on a short time crunch because the asshole's next shipment of girls is coming up, and I need to somehow kill him, then save those females.

I was kind of hoping to see some evidence of where he keeps them in the house, but that was just wishful thinking. I knew this shit wasn't going to be easy and I knew frying a big fish like Henry would be fucking difficult.

Admittedly, I didn't think the pervy fucker would have such a hot fucking son and if this situation were completely different, he'd be exactly my type. The second I saw him I knew I could climb that fucker like a tree. But just the thought of him being anything like daddy dearest sours the sentiment instantly.

I start my shower and wait for this cheap ass apartment to spew out the hot water. My savings are beginning to run out and I know I need to wrap this up as soon as possible.

I peel myself out of the leather outfit and step into the hot water. I still can't get the sight of Henry's son out of my mind, the way his throat worked when swallowing the water, or his abs glistening with sweat, and that voice, all gruff and angry.

The hot water cascades over my body and I lift my foot to press into the tub's edge. It's been a while since I've even cared about my own needs, always about the men I must kill, and never getting myself off.

My fingers skim down over my large breasts, giving my nipple a tweak on the way, and down my soft belly to settle over my mound. My heart rate kicks up and I run my fingers through my folds. I moan, tipping my head back and feeling the water rush over my face, the feeling refreshing.

I circle my clit and think of Henry's son, those dark angry eyes, and rough voice. I feel myself grow wet and slide two fingers inside, working myself exactly how I like it.

My other hand comes up and tugs at my nipple, sending tingles straight to my pussy. I can't erase his face from my brain and it's perplexing to be masturbating to a sick son of a bitch, but I can't stop myself now.

My thumb hits my clit as my fingers dance inside of me, brushing that spot I know will send me over the edge quickly.

I can feel my wetness coating my hand and I rub myself back and forth, my lower belly beginning to tighten. I wish I were riding his dick and I wish his father were watching it all happen. Then, when I was done, I would slice both of their throats and bathe in their blood.

That thought has me tumbling over the edge as visions of Henry gripping his bloody throat and his son screaming for mercy floods my senses.

My pussy contracts around my fingers and my release continues as I imagine the warm water is their blood, spraying over my face.

That is a first, I have never gotten off to a victim and the fantasy of their deaths but I may make it a fucking routine now.

I finish up in the shower and pad my way over to the papers scattered on my desk. Thank god I'm fucking relaxed after that shower because looking at this shit shows me just how much work I have.

Time to get this fucking show on the road.

Chapter Seven

Selene

I pull an all nighter, mapping out the obnoxiously large mansion and marking as many things as I can remember about the layout. Every door I walked through, every stupid painting, everything.

I mutter to myself as my feet throb from the walk home, cursing out the rude cunt for the millionth time for not bringing me home. I don't want him knowing where I live, but he could have dropped me a lot fucking closer to home instead of expecting me to walk.

I flick through some papers I've scribbled on recently, double checking his movements and actions I've noticed through the week. I add that his son obviously lives at home, which is annoying as fuck, but not a complete issue. If I'm lucky, I can get the pair of the rich cunts in one go, I just have to play it smart.

I stash everything away before grabbing my shoes and calling an Uber, wandering outside to wait for it on the curb.

My day is planned out well.

I'll have breakfast at the diner in town to wake my ass up properly, I need to buy a new dress for my next meet with Henry, and then the local bar is calling my name. I really need a fucking stiff drink.

I indulge a little too much on breakfast, knowing it'll hurt the bank, but I'm fucking starving, so it's worth it. Especially when they bring out my plate that's piled high with eggs, bacon, and toast. The coffee is a gift from the gods, too.

I take my time eating, scoping out the other customers and keeping my ears open for anything interesting. It is amazing how many people talk about shit that they shouldn't, making my life a hell of a lot easier.

Now that I feel slightly human again, I walk the short distance across the street to the department store, browsing through the stunning dresses until my eyes land on a tight thigh high black dress. It's dipped low in the back, and the moment I try it on, I know it's the one.

It makes my tits look fucking amazing, and once I add some heels to the outfit, my legs will look fucking stunning, too.

I guess all I need now is a drink.

I wander further down the street to the bar, surveying the room as I sit on a stool and order a drink. I'm aware of the drunken sleazebag beside me, but I blatantly ignore him and sip my whiskey, scanning the room again before turning my attention back to my drink.

"Hey, you look lonely, doll face," Sleazebag slurs, almost falling off his bar stool as he leans closer. The smell of whiskey and cigarettes is sickeningly strong on his breath, and I fight the urge to gag.

"I'm talking to you, you stuck up bitch!" He growls when I continue to ignore him, my eyes finally sliding to his as I cock my head a fraction.

"I was hoping you'd get the picture and take a hike," I say sweetly, his bloodshot eyes narrowing.

"Fucking slut!" He spits out, staggering to his feet to try and tower over me. If I were going to run away from the asshole, his breath would have done it, not his height. He is barely five and a half feet tall.

He jabs his fat finger into my chest, stumbling slightly as he belches in my face.

"You think you're too good for me?" He demands, and I let out a light laugh.

"I know for a fucking fact that I am. Like I said, take a hike, asshole."

I brace myself as he throws himself at me, almost knocking me off balance, but a hand comes out of nowhere and grabs the back of the guy's shirt, hauling him back sharply. Before the drunken dick-bag can react, a fist hits his face just before the side of his head is slammed down onto the bar.

My eyes flick over to my defender, and I'm surprised as fuck to see the rich asshole's son standing there, holding the guy down by the back of the neck as he struggles.

"Hank, the fuck have I told you about attacking women who don't want your shriveled-up dick? Apologize. Now," he demands, surprising me further. I was unaware the prick even knew the word apologize.

The man stutters, rambling on about some random crap, but

Zander growls loudly, slamming him down again.

"Hank, I'm not fucking around."

"Sorry, Miss," the man who's apparently named Hank blurts out, stumbling away the moment he's let go. Cowardly piece of shit.

Zander's eyes skim over me before his lips kick up into a cruel smirk.

"You're the paid whore that Henry brought home yesterday."

I quirk an eyebrow, grabbing my drink and downing it before replying.

"I haven't taken any money from Mr. Walton, so the name calling is a little unnecessary if you ask me," I say dryly, but he snorts and leans against the bar, not taking his eyes off me.

"No one was asking you."

I turn my attention back to the bar, flagging the bartender down to pour me another drink, but Zander's eyes are burning a hole in the side of my head, so I struggle to keep my no fucks given attitude in place. All I can think about is him bending me over the fucking bar and ploughing himself into my pussy, spectators be damned.

When I don't give him another glance, he crosses his arms and speaks again, his voice rough.

"Are you honestly sitting here alone? Let me guess, you're looking for your next client?"

I down most of my fresh drink and shrug.

"I wanted a drink, so I'm having one. Why do you care? I can handle myself," I say curtly as annoyance takes over his features.

"I don't give a fuck what happens to you, I was just calling you out for being stupid. This place is probably teeming with herpes, so have at it," he grits out, his fingers twitching by his side as he uncrosses his arms.

"Makes all the sense that you're here. Anyway, I was thirsty and I have things to do, so I'd better be on my way. Please tell Henry I said hello, Sir," I answer smoothly, standing and turning to leave but his voice stops me.

"Don't call me 'Sir', I'm not my father and I'm sure as shit not middle aged. I'm Zander," he grunts out, and I'm not sure who is more surprised, me or him.

I give him a soft smile, reaching out to touch his arm lightly on my way past him.

"Well, Zander, please tell your father I said hello," then I walk out, making sure to sway my hips as I go.

    I feel his burning gaze on me until I close the door behind me.

Chapter Eight

Zander

"Fuuuuck, who's the walking wet dream?" Santos asks as I join the guys in the back at a booth. I'm fucking sure the horny bastard has unlimited cum and stamina because he literally just blew his load down some slut's throat out in the side alley when we arrived.

I still can't believe I fucking helped that dumb slut Selene, let alone actually gave her my name. The fuck is wrong with me?

I shake the thoughts of her out of my head, giving Santos a bored glance.

"She's nobody, just some paid whore Henry brought home yesterday," I reply, taking a drink from Darius who smirks at me.

"Paid whore, huh? Get her digits from your dad so I can throw some dough her way. I want her trussed up in my bed pronto. She has the perfect pale skin to mark with my ropes."

"You'd really stick your dick in something that Henry's banging? Dude, c'mon. Have a little bit of dignity," I scoff, but Santos laughs like a fucking hyena, his gaze jumping between me and Darius.

"I'd sure as shit fuck her. She's hot as sin, and I bet she'll scream real pretty against my blade. You honestly wouldn't tap that? You should hit her up and see if you can get a family deal going on since Henry's boning her, but then tell her we're all cousins so we get a discount too."

I have no idea how to handle him some days.

"So what if she's hot? I don't want to fuck her," I snort, but Darius grins and nudges Santos.

"I say we fuck her. Wanna tag team?" Jesus fucking Christ.

Blaze watches them silently as they plot their next sexcapade, but he finally looks up at me and smirks cruelly, the scar stretching on his face slightly with the motion.

"Just get her number and let them have her since you don't want her. Besides, if they scare her enough, you won't have to worry about seeing her in your house again. The best way to get a bitch to never come back, is to let Santos' crazy ass near them."

The man has a point, but something nags at me, making me scowl. I don't want them to scare her to death, and the thought of never having her in the house again sucks.

There's something strange about her, and I'm a curious kind of guy. The guys are right, too. I do want to fuck her, but there is no way in hell that I'll let my dick get anywhere near a cunt my dad has been in.

Wait, what if she ends up being my stepmom? I can't handle that idea at all. Apart from being pissed at Henry for moving on so fast, I don't want Selene under my dad's firm hand.

He's messed me up, so fuck knows what he'll do to her.

He'll break her, and I don't think she has any idea about what she's messing with.

"Earth to Zander! Where the fuck did you go, asshole? You in wet pussy land with your pin dick again?" Darius exclaims as he snaps his fingers in my face, drawing me back to the conversation. I didn't mean to zone out like that.

Santos grins, practically bouncing in his seat.

"So, you gonna let us play with her? You sure you don't wanna play with her cunt before I get my hands on it? Can't promise I won't break her," he says with glee, high fiving Darius as I sigh and motion towards them with my hand.

"Just don't break her too quickly, alright? I wanna figure out if she's just sex to Henry, or if he's got his eyes on her a little closer to home. She claims she's never received money from him. I don't like the idea of some bitch becoming my new mommy when the cunt looks younger than me," I grumble, causing Darius to groan and rub his dick through his pants with no shame. He's a lower level of crazy compared to Santos, but the fucker is still twisted.

"I'm gonna get her to call me daddy while she's bouncing on my dick. Fuck, I bet it would be hot as fuck coming from those lips when she's breathless. Santos, we gotta make her call us daddy."

"If the cunt's speaking, she's not screaming. I don't give a fuck what she calls you, but she's gonna be screaming and bleeding for me," Santos smirks, not hiding his excitement as it flashes in his eyes.

I hope you're ready, Selene.
My boys are coming for you.

REAPED

THE REAPER INCARNATE

Chapter Nine

Selene

I can't believe that piece of shit Walton Jr. was at the fucking bar. I didn't see that coming, and now I'm going to have to add watching him to the list.

Zander. I knew his name before today, of course, having stalked the fuck out of his father, but there weren't any recent pictures of him I could find online, and he and his father didn't seem to like to be around each other, save for when they're trading people.

I get inside my little apartment and throw the dress onto my threadbare couch, heading straight for my bottle of whiskey. Now I have to play the waiting game, if Henry wants me, he has my number, and it needs to be him that wants me. Then all of this can really take off.

I need to release the pent up anger I have for Zander and his peekaboo act today, I think a late night shift at my unconventional fucking job sounds nice. I pull out a thick manilla envelope from under my couch cushions and open it up.

Inside is a compilation of hits I need to get through this year and as thick as it is now, it was once twice as large. I've been a busy fucking girl.

I hold up the first paper and grin. Looks like I'll be paying a certain gynecologist a visit.

This man Dr. Carl Ignis likes to touch women inappropriately and then rapes them for good measure. A few women have come forward but it's always been shut down due to no evidence and Dr. Ignis being an upstanding citizen with a family at home.

Dr. Ignis is a piece of shit and I can't wait to get my hands bloody.

I dress in a pair of black skinny jeans and a white crop top, pairing it with my trench. Carl likes to peruse the few blocks that's known for young prostitutes and seedy drug deals. It's Friday, so let's see if Carl comes out to play.

I'm fucking walking around in these fucking boots again but I can't help how much I enjoy the connection to Pretty Woman and I'll gladly take the pain. A few of the girls I know call out to me and a few others screw up their faces, there's no in between.

"Have any of you seen the gyno yet?" I ask a few standing under a streetlamp.

"Dr. Ignis hasn't come by yet," his regular giggles. Sorry bitch, the cunt is mine tonight.

About two hours pass and I have ignored about four different guys, then I see him. He drives a white Range Rover and slows down when he sees his regular girl. Can't have that.

I walk right up to his passenger window as he's lowering it.

"I want you." I tell him, leaning forward into the window.

"Really?" His shit brown eyes shine bright and eager.

"Yes. I've been waiting for hours," I let my pouty mouth curl up into a slow smile. "Don't keep me waiting any longer."

His tongue snakes out and runs along his thin lips as he combs his fingers through his thinning blonde hair.

"Get in," he says and I smile wider.

Got you, bitch.

"Dr. Ignis," his regular calls out. "Will you be back later?"

"He won't be back later," I close the door and lean out of the window. "Find a new regular."

Carl chuckles from beside me, thinking a pair of whores are fighting over him, but in reality I'm telling her he ain't coming back because he'll soon be choking on his own blood.

He takes us to a deserted mall parking lot and parks the vehicle, looking over at me expectantly.

"Tell me what you want," I grin at him and lower my lashes.

"How much will this cost me?" He runs his finger over his fish thin lips. "And are you old enough to be doing this?"

"Tonight's on me and would it matter?"

"No." He shakes his head. "It wouldn't matter."

I know, Carl. You just want pussy no matter the age.

"Undo your pants and let me get acquainted with you."

He does as I ask and when he pulls out his thin noodle dick, I try my best not to laugh. No wonder he turns to prostitutes and unwilling patients, the man's got nothing down below. He's even hard, clearly not impressive.

"Oh!" I say excitedly, "look at this cock. I can't wait to have it choking me."

He grins and leans back further in his seat. Stupid fucker. I'll be lucky if the fucking thing reaches my throat. I've slurped ramen thicker than him.

I lean forward and wrap my small hand around him, choking back a laugh as my fingers meet. I spit down onto his head and begin to jack him off, there's no way I'm sucking him off without a condom because this fucker likes to stick his little friend into just about anything.

"Is this how you like it?" I ask him.

"Oh yeah," he groans.

"Would you rather I go slower, faster, or what if I was saying no?"

"Huh?" He's only half paying attention.

"Yeah," I lift my head up and stop my movements. "Do you prefer me unwilling? Isn't that what you do with the girls you rape in your office?"

His eyes widen and then his eyebrows crash together in immediate anger.

"What the fuck did you say?" He growls.

There he is.

"I said," I tighten my hold around his toothpick dick. "Don't you like sticking this itty bitty cock into unwilling participants?"

He grabs a fistful of my hair, bringing my face away from his dick, and I swing my fist into his nose. He's not expecting it and the spray of blood lands all over my face.

"What the fuck?" He yells, releasing my hair and grabbing his nose with both hands.

"Dr. Ignis has been a naughty boy," I tsk and pull my knife from my pocket, switching open the blade. "Let's play a game. I'll ask you questions and for every wrong answer I get to stab you."

"You're a fucking lunatic!" He screams and reaches for the door handle.

"Wrong answer." I sing-song and stab him in his side.

"Stop!" He pants, gripping his side.

"How many girls have you raped?"

"Fuck you!" He spits, and I wiggle in my seat with excitement.

"Another one!" I squeal and stab him in his thigh. His scream of agony washes over me and I moan at the sound.

"Stop." His words are a bit slower. "You will be going away for a long time."

"How many girls did you threaten after raping them?" I point the tip of my blade at him.

He watches it warily and reaches his hand once again for the door handle.

"Stop it." His bloody fingers slip on the metal.

"You're not going to be truthful, huh?" I snicker. "Looks like I'm wasting a perfectly good night."

Before he can say anything else, I stab the knife through his throat, and watch as he tries to get a grip on it, choking through his blood.

"When you get to Hell, Dr. Ignis, warn the devil I'm coming." I pull out the knife and coat my hand in the blood.

I press my blood soaked finger to his forehead and hum as I draw the Reaper's scythe.

Chapter Ten

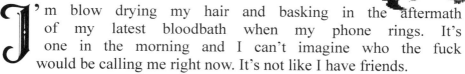

I'm blow drying my hair and basking in the aftermath of my latest bloodbath when my phone rings. It's one in the morning and I can't imagine who the fuck would be calling me right now. It's not like I have friends.

I hold up the phone screen and smile when I see Henry Walton's name.

"Hello?" I pick up, making sure I sound breathless.

"Selene." His voice is low and commanding.

"Yes, Sir?" I coat my words in innocence and grin when he catches his breath.

"I want to see you."

"Now?" I act surprised.

"Yes, I'm sending you a car to bring you here. What's your address?" Fucking bossy asshole.

"I'll meet them at the same spot as last time." No way will he ever get my address.

"You have twenty minutes." Then he hangs up.

Sounds like a grumpy someone needs a good cock banging and I need to pretend I'm fucking enjoying it.

I head into my bedroom and pull out a short jersey dress, then pile my hair on top of my head. Time to look a little younger and tempt Walton into doing naughty things to me. I need to gain his trust so that I can find out where he keeps his shipments and how often he gets them.

I walk to the same corner as our last pick up and sure enough the same Rolls Royce is there idling on the side. As soon as the driver sees me, he gets out and opens the back door.

"Hi." I smile at him and get a stern nod in return.

Looks like he could deal with a good cock banging, too.

I get comfortable in the back seat and stifle a yawn into my hand. I was looking forward to a good sleep after gutting Carl, and now I need to act like a good little whore. I doubt Henry wants a sleepy one.

We pull through a set of familiar gates and the driver stops in front of the entrance. I wait for my door to be opened and by the time I step out, Henry is waiting. Eager much?

"Hello, Selene." His voice makes me want to puke in his mouth.

"Hello, Sir." I smile through my nausea as his mouth pulls back into a wide smile.

He holds out his arm, ushering me inside, and I step through the threshold. Is Zander here tonight? I look around the foyer, hoping to see his scowling face, for what reason, I don't have the slightest clue. Maybe I want him to see me about to fuck his father.

"Would you like some wine?" Henry asks.

"No, I want to suck your cock again." I don't have all night and I really want to get back home to sleep.

He chokes on my answer and quickly regains his composure. "Good answer."

I bet it is, Dickface Walton.

He leads me into an office and slams the door behind us. He really is fucking eager.

"Get up on my desk and spread your legs, I want your pussy in my mouth," he demands and I do just as he asks.

I will never say no to having my fucking pussy eaten out, that's fucking blasphemy. I spread my legs and show the old bastard that I forgot to put on a pair of panties.

"Oh fuck," he groans and kneels in front of me.

"Please make me come, Sir."

He growls and grabs my thighs in each hand before he buries his head into my pussy. Henry is a fucking douchebag but the fucker can eat a pussy. He's not shy of the asshole and shows my rear hole some love, too. I thread my fingers through his hair and pull it tighter. I'm craving this release.

As soon as I feel that telltale tightening, I begin to rub my clit along his nose, and he fucks me with his tongue.

"Fuck yes, Sir." I moan.

I tip my head back and groan through my release, stuffing his head in tighter. I hope the fucker dies of suffocation.

He comes up and I watch as he licks his wet lips, my juices all over his chin.

"You missed some." I say as I lean forward, running my finger along his chin, and sucking it into my mouth. "Mmm."

"Get down and lean over the desk," his gruff voice orders me. Looks like I'm getting a dick down.

"Yes, Sir."

I hop down and turn around, slowly leaning over. I hear the crinkle of a condom wrapper and then he's flipping my skirt up and slamming inside of me. Thankfully, I was wet because he is rough and fast. I moan when the tip of his cock hits a certain spot inside of me and I begin to imagine it's Zander fucking me, not his father.

His fingers dig into my hips and his balls slap against my clit, making me begin to tighten again. Fuck, he really does know how to work this cock and the more I think about Zander's abs, I'm rushing towards a second orgasm.

"You like this cock don't you, you fucking whore." Here we go. "Take it like the dirty piece of shit you are. How many cocks have been in your cunt today?"

"Only yours, Sir." I moan as he becomes rougher.

"You lying dirty bitch." He snarls and grabs my hair, yanking my head back. "How much cum have you swallowed today?"

I moan as I clench around his dick and my eyes close as I come, seeing visions of Zander fucking me hard.

"You filthy whore," he slaps my ass hard. "Tight pussy whore."

He groans and slams inside of me one final time, cumming finally, then he pulls out quickly and I turn to watch him chuck the condom into the wastebasket, landing beside a few others. Gross.

"Could I get that drink now?" I ask him.

He nods and pulls his pants up, giving me an evil grin. "Worked you up to a thirst, huh?"

"Oh yes." I nod. Get the fuck out of the room.

He's striding out a few moments later and I quickly look at my surroundings. There's not much I can do since he has a camera in the upper right corner, sick perv probably makes videos of all the women he brings in here.

There's a painting of an older man sitting over the mantle of the fireplace and it's sitting slightly askew, like maybe it's moved often. Henry walks back in and sees me looking at the painting.

"That's my father," he hands me the water. "He started our business from nothing."

Just a couple of girls back then I bet.

"He's handsome," I look at him. "I see where you get it from."

"The car is waiting for you out front." He tells me.

Thank God.

"Thank you." I nod and follow him to the front door.

"I'll call you again, Selene." He grasps my chin in his hand.

"Goodnight, Sir." His eyes flash and then he nods, stalking back inside.

I can't wait to go home and relive this, only with his son is his place.

Chapter Eleven

Zander

I can smell her.

She has somehow taken over my massive fucking house with her scent, and the moment my dick stirs I demand it go back down.

I can't let her get to me, no way in fucking hell. She's just a prostitute for fuck's sake, nothing special.

My dick disagrees though like the treacherous bastard that it is.

I make my way through the kitchen and up to my room, becoming angrier as more of her scent consumes me. She is fucking everywhere.

I grab the back of my shirt in my hand and pull it over my head, throwing it on the floor as I make my way towards my bathroom to shower. I kick my pants off, along with my boxers before reaching for the taps and turning the water to scalding hot.

Maybe burning my balls off will set me straight.

I climb under the spray and close my eyes, trying to remove the pretty blue eyed hooker from my thoughts.

Fuck, now I'm hard.

I consider my options for a second then grasp my throbbing dick in my hand, stroking it firmly a few times before resting my forearm against the shower wall, leaning my forehead against it.

I pump my fist faster, a small groan leaving me at the building pleasure. I don't have to wait long once I picture Selene on her knees, her eyes staring up at me as she swallows my dick deep, her wavy blonde hair wrapped firmly around my fist.

Heat tingles down my spine as my balls tighten, causing me to grunt and slow my hand as hot cum jets from my dick and hits the shower wall.

I stand there for a moment not moving, needing to steady myself from the intensity of it. I swear I haven't cum that hard in my fucking life.

I finally rinse the evidence of my weak moment from the wall before rinsing my body and turning the water off, stepping out to grab a towel. I'm not expecting Blaze to be leaning against the sink with his arms crossed and his signature scowl on his face. I didn't even hear him come in.

"Well, that was fucking disgusting," he comments, but the ghost of a smile tugs at his lips.

I wrap the towel around my waist and snort, frowning at him with annoyance.

"You didn't have to watch, asshole. I'm in my fucking bathroom, it's not like I did it in the kitchen."

Seriously, I can't even jack off in my own fucking bathroom any more without someone complaining?

His eyebrow quirks up, amusement filling his eyes. Well, it's as close to amusement as it gets. Blaze is way too serious all the time.

"She's getting to you more than you let on, Zander."

"Who?" I grumble, moving into my room with him hot on my heels.

"The whore your dad's fucking," he grunts as if I'm stupid.

I stare at him for a moment before grabbing some boxers and quickly pulling them on.

"I haven't thought about the cunt, why would she be getting to me?" I bite out, but he smirks, cocking his head at me.

"You said Selene when you nutted. That's her name, isn't it?"

Fuck.

I go to speak but he rolls his eyes and cuts me off.

"I think it's a dumb idea but fuck her and get her out of your system or something. You need to get to her before Darius and Santos do, or there's going to be nothing left for you to stick your dick in. Fuck her, then let them have her. I meant what I said earlier, man. You won't have to see her again once those two get their hands on her. Fuck her, then get your head in the game."

"She's just a paid slut that Henry likes to blow in. She's nothing more than a cum bucket, so it's not like she's messing me up. My head's in the game, I promise," I grit out, not liking this conversation in the slightest.

He scoffs, giving me a dirty look. If looks could kill, I'd be six feet under right now.

"That's the problem, Zander. The other two are always running loose and fucking shit up, but you're more levelheaded. You've been off with the fucking fairies all afternoon, and now you're in here jerking on your dick to that cunt?" He snaps.

"My heads fucking fine, Blaze. You have nothing to worry about," I argue, but he just glares at me, his voice low.

"No? I was in your room when you got home and you didn't even notice, let alone when I walked into the bathroom. Like I said, go and fill her cunt up with your cum, then get your ass into gear before you end up fucking hurt or dead. Anyone could have been in the house tonight instead of me, and you weren't observant enough to even notice. Is her pussy really worth your fucking life?" He snarks, turning and stalking from the room, leaving me standing there like a fucking idiot.

Bad thing is, I am starting to want a piece of that pussy and I can't seem to shake it off.

I let Blaze go, not wanting to deal with his fucking drama any longer. I climb into bed and grab my phone, scrolling through my contacts until I find her name.

I shouldn't have taken her number from Dad's phone, but it's for Santos and Darius, not me. Well, it's not supposed to be for me, but my fingers twitch with the temptation to send her a text.

Instead, I copy the contact details and send them to Santos, turning my phone off for the night and rolling over to sleep before I can regret my decision.

Too late.

REAPED

THE REAPER INCARNATE

Chapter Twelve

Selene

My phone beeps as a text comes through, and I frown at the unknown number. I'm a little surprised when I open it to discover it's one of Zander's friends.

He literally said hello and that his name was 'Santos, Zander's hot friend'.

Fucking wacko.

I finish my morning coffee before replying, not sure why he's even texting me to begin with. I don't have to wonder for long after asking him what he wants. He wants to do some business with me.

Well, with my pussy.

I can't tell him no, because it will fuck up my cover, but I don't want to get involved with them. The further away I stay, the better, because the moment Henry Walton is dead and cold, I'm going for his son.

I can't have people seeing me around them too much.

I groan when he sends another text after a while, an address showing up on the screen with a time. He's having a party apparently, and he wants my pussy to keep his dick company.

Just wonderful.

There's no way out of this without raising questions, so I thank him for the invite and say I'll think about it. It could be a good idea to get closer to Zander and his father, so I know I have to go. Luckily, I have a few hours to get ready.

I have a shower and shave everything, before climbing out to blow dry my hair. I decide to straighten it before applying my make-up, giving my eyes a smoky effect to make them pop.

Then I grab the black dress I bought the other day and hesitate before putting it on. I originally bought it to lure Henry a little more, but I want to see Zander's expression when he sees me in it for some fucked up reason. The guy is taking over all my fucking brain cells, and it's driving me mental.

I slip on some strappy black heels, showing off my lean calf muscles and long legs, my ass nearly sticking out the bottom of the dress as I turn in front of the mirror to see my handy work. I have to admit, I look good.

I'd fuck me.

Glancing at my phone to check the time, I realize I'm already late, so I call an Uber and find my purse before wandering down to the street for my ride.

I know I'm at the right house when the driver pulls up on the curb and I can hear music thumping from inside as people spill out of the side door, drinking and smoking.

I swing my legs out the door, only to have a shadow fall over me.

My eyes dart up and I find myself staring at an angry dude with a scar down his face, his scowl giving him a mean look. It's kind of hot in a scary way.

"He seriously invited you?" He asks as if he can't believe it, my eyes narrowing in defense.

"Santos did, yeah. Why?"

Something crosses his dark eyes before his lip twitches, as if fighting a smile.

"Oh, did he now? Hope you're ready then, because this is going to be the worst night of your fucking life. I can't believe that fucker actually invited you, this is hilarious," he grunts, not seeming like it's as funny as he says.

He steps aside and lets me out of the Uber, but when I turn to speak to him again, he's already halfway towards the booming house party. I'm not surprised really, he's a bit of a dick.

I make my way up to the house, letting myself inside and almost getting bowled over by Zander who looks murderous.

"He seriously fucking invited you?" He demands as if I'm lying, causing me to take a small step back in surprise. I regain my ground and take a step almost against him, my pussy pulsing as his scent hits my nose and my chest brushes against his firm body.

"Where's Santos? Why do you care?" I ask, his eyes boring into mine with hate.

"He's in the back room. I told that fucker not to invite you," he spits, confusion and annoyance washing through me. I want to punch him in the face, but then I'll feel obligated to kiss it better. Not today, motherfucker.

I cross my arms, causing my chest to pop out and draw his attention.

"What's the big deal? I'm working, so…"

"So you're just here to make a quick buck? Or are you here to suss me out some more?" He demands, towering over me until my back is pressed against the door.

Fuck, he's onto me.

"Zander, I'm not here to be a bother to you. Santos invited me, so I said I'd show up. That's it. Why would I need to suss you out?" I laugh lightly, kicking myself for the situation I'm currently in. He's getting suspicious.

"You don't think I know what you're doing? Worming your way into my rich dad's pocket like you are? You trying to get to know me so you can try some of that step-mommy bullshit with me?" He argues, but his hands absently hang by my side, his fingers lightly brushing against the thin fabric of my dress. My heart rate spikes as his eyes darken, but he gets hold of himself as I clear my throat and push him back a step.

"I'm not a gold digger, and I sure as shit am not looking for a husband, if that's what you're implying. It's strictly business, that's it. I'm too young to be your fucking mommy anyways," I say defensively, his features cooling slightly.

"How old are you?"

"Twenty five. I'd prefer to earn my money on my knees, than let someone just pay for my shit. Don't act like you know me, asshole, because you fucking don't," I murmur before slipping away from him. I startle as I walk into the back room and instantly get shoved lightly against a wall.

The guy looks certifiably crazy, but he is hot as fuck. He presses himself against me, his tongue tracing his lips as he watches me with a smirk.

"Hey, Selene, right?"

"Santos?" I ask with a small smile, his eyes shining at me knowing his name.

"That's me. I was going to get you to blow me while I do lines with the guys, but I don't particularly want them to see you enjoying me so much. You know, because they'll get jealous."

I don't even get a word out before his lips are on my neck, a gasp leaving me as his teeth bite firmly into my soft skin. I'm starting to second guess my decision to show up. He looks ready to fuck me and kill me at the same time, and I have no idea how to handle that.

I press my palms against his stomach to push him back, but I hesitate as I feel the solid abs beneath the shirt. My fingers trace the grooves of his muscles, and he chuckles in my ear.

"You like what you're feeling? Wait until I get you naked, you'll be screaming for me," he practically whispers in my ear, sending tingles down my spine.

Someone grabs my hand and gently tugs me aside, causing Santos to scowl.

"Darius, fuck off. She's mine right now."

Darius rolls his eyes but smiles at me, his voice as smooth as silk as he tucks my hair behind my ear.

"I'm Darius, and you're fucking hot. Do you allow, let's say, multiple people in a business transaction?" He asks as if we were swapping pantry goods, my mouth going dry for some reason. Both guys are hot as hell, but there is something off about them too, I just can't place what it is.

I give him a coy smile, fluttering my lashes at him.

"I don't know what you're talking about. I just wanted to come to the party since I had a night off."

He chuckles, his eyes lighting up, knowing I'm full of complete shit.

"How about you join me and Santos upstairs and we will show you how to fucking party then?"

When I don't answer him instantly, he swoops down and kisses the living shit out of me, and I can't hold back the moan as he sandwiches me between him and Santos, who groans and rubs the hard bulge in his pants against my ass.

"Fuck, man. Throw her over your shoulder and let's get this started."

Someone screams from the other room, and Zander runs in like his ass is on fire.

"Get everyone out, now. Antonio's guys just fucking showed up!" He shouts, Darius moving back from me instantly and pulling a gun out of the back of his pants, while Santos is already demanding people to fuck off out the back door. They scatter because that fucker is one crazy son of a bitch. Half his words are coming out in Spanish, and he's waving his own gun around like a crackhead at the local gas station.

A gunshot rings out through the house, and Scar Face storms in with a semi-automatic rifle and rage all over his face. Something tells me the fucker is never happy, even if he has his dick buried in the best pussy in the world, the cunt will still glare at them.

"Fuck me, this bitch is still here? Fine, fuck. Can you shoot?" Scar guy asks me, offering me a handgun without waiting for my answer. I much prefer my knife, but you don't bring a knife to a gun fight, so it will have to do.

Zander's glaring at his friend like he's crazy, when the actual crazy friend is jumping up and down while laughing.

"Fuck yeah, all bets are off since he's brought this shit to my house, motherfuckers," Santos laughs, his eyes darting around between them all as if he needs permission to let loose.

Darius glances at Scar Face who grunts, motioning to the door.

"Yeah man, it's your house, go crazy."

Santos lets out a hyena laugh, making pew pew noises as he darts down the hallway, causing Darius to chuckle before following him, glancing over his shoulder to wink at me.

"I'll finish this then get back to finishing you, deal?"

I giggle, hating the sound that leaves my mouth, but he flashes me a bright smile and goes to help his friend, leaving me with the angry dude and Zander who looks just as pissed.

He eyes my weapon and snorts.

"Do you even know how to use that thing?"

"Of course I do. I'm a prostitute in this shithole. I'd be stupid not to know how to defend myself," I snap, hating it when men assume I'm defenseless and need saving all the goddamn time.

Before he can stop me, I stalk after Santos and Darius, my eyes landing on a heavily tattooed guy in the kitchen. He grins at me, cracking his knuckles.

"Just what I fucking wanted, a portable cum dump. The guys will like you. Put the gun down and come here, I won't hurt you unlike these assholes," he croons, and I can't stop the fucking eye roll.

Is he for real right now?

I lift my gun and cock my head.

"Why do guys think I'm worried about getting hurt, when I'm

usually the biggest monster in the room?" I question, confusion flashing in his eyes before I smirk and pull the trigger, his nose splattering as blood sprays from the wound. He drops like a sack of shit, but a deep groan comes from him, telling me he's still alive.

I silently dart across the room and slit his throat with my knife, creeping through the next room and towards another door, flinging it open to find another guy has somehow managed to get his arm around Santos' neck.

The door opening distracts him enough for Santos to break free, but the fucker keeps getting in my way as I follow the guy with my gun. After a few seconds, I scowl.

"Fuck's sake, asshole. Duck!" I shout, Santos turning instantly, his eyes going wide for a second before he drops to the ground and out of my way.

I grab my knife again and throw it across the room, the blade lodging in the guy's forehead just as Darius joins us, his face and chest covered in blood.

The room goes quiet as the guy drops to the floor, and I tsk as I walk over to him and put my foot on his head, yanking my blade out.

"What an idiot. I even warned him that I was going to get him because I told you to duck. Are all men so fucking stupid?" I ask, turning to face them to see them both staring at me, mouths open.

Santos has a raging boner, but I'm not surprised. Crazy, remember?

Zander and the other asshole jog in as we hear car tires screaming away from the house, and Darius points at me as if it were all my fault.

"She did it."

"She saved my ass. Now I'm horny as fuck, and I'm about to start humping the couch cushions. Fuck, my dick is seriously fucking hard right now. Did you see that Darius? She got him smack bang in the forehead!" Santos exclaims, not hesitating to wrap his arms around my waist and spin me around, kissing me hard. Death seems to make me horny too, so I moan into his mouth and don't fight him off, despite the audience.

I'm yanked back hard, and Zander glares at Santos as if he has the right to.

"We have shit to clean up, and you are not going to leave it with us while you fuck her in victory. Get to work. Blaze, run her home," Zander orders, but Scar Face scoffs.

"I'm not taking her anywhere. She can't fucking leave after what just happened. Are you stupid?"

My back stiffens as anger rolls through me.

"You can't keep me here, jackass. I killed two people, so why would I say anything?!" I shout, but his angry eyes land on mine and he sneers.

"Because no bitch knows how to kill a guy like that, let alone without remorse. You barely even blinked at it, so you're not just some hooker slut from the city, you're trained to fucking kill."

Oh, fuck.

REAPED

THE REAPER INCARNATE

Chapter Thirteen

Zander

"I don't give a shit if she's trained, that just makes me wanna fuck her even more. Seriously, she threw a fucking knife at him from across the room and got a bullseye! Please let me keep her, she's perfect!" Santos begs, grinding my gears a fraction.

I've never known the fucker to be so fucking obsessed with a chick before, but since she saved him in a bloodied way, he wants her right or wrong.

Blaze shakes his head, glaring at our friend.

"The fuck is wrong with you? Other than the obvious. She might be a fucking spy for all we know. We can't have her fucking up our plans!" He hisses.

I watch Blaze for a moment before sighing, rubbing my temples with frustration.

"She's right, you know? We can't keep her locked up here."

"Says fucking who? I thought you would have loved the opportunity to be locked up with her, Zan. Go get her out of your system while you can," Blaze snaps, causing Santos' eyes to dart to him with a frown.

"Hey! I get her! She distracted that dude until I broke free, then she…"

"I'm aware she saved you and killed the guy with a knife. We've been going over this for nearly an hour, dick head. Zander wants her, so let him have her," Blaze grunts, all eyes going to me with confusion.

I count to three in my head, needing to compose myself before speaking.

"She stays tonight, then we take her home tomorrow and suss out her house, alright? No one fucks her until we know who she fucking is and who she works for, got it?" I say calmly, making Santos scowl and throw complaints at me in the process, but Blaze gives me a nod, agreeing with me. I can always rely on him to side with me.

I have to admit though, I'm surprised that Selene got involved in any of it and didn't run the moment she could. If I thought she consumed all my thoughts before, she sure as fuck did now.

Who the fuck is she?

"I don't want her to go, I like her! She obviously likes me if she'll kill a guy for me!" Santos continues to argue, draining some of my willpower.

"We talk to her tomorrow about it all, alright? Tonight she stays until we can get some information out of her. You and Darius stay here, Blaze and I will go and see what we can find out," I mutter, both of them groaning at me.

They'd end up fucking her if we let them go and interrogate her without supervision.

I head back out to the back room where we left Darius in charge of the little imp and find them in a heated argument.

"I am not fucking staying here!" She screams and lifts her gun to me as we walk in.

"Whoa," I raise my hands. "Chill. We have a few questions about what just went down."

"I saved your useless fucking lives," she sneers. "I should've fucking ran when I had the chance instead."

Okay, so she's pissed and understandably. But I need to know why the fuck a weapon trained hooker is fucking my father.

"She's pissed," Darius echoes my thoughts and grabs his cock through his jeans. "Fuck, I really like her pissed."

"Same," Santos pipes up behind me. "Baby, we really like you pissed."

She rolls her eyes but I see a ghost of a smile hover around her lips.

"Listen, I like to suck and fuck cock," she shrugs. "But men tend to think a female deserves to be beaten or raped instead, all of what you saw was self-taught."

Nope, not buying it.

"Look, it's late as fuck. We're gonna clean up and crash." I look into her bright blue eyes. "Please stay here so we can talk in the morning."

"Do I have a fucking choice?" She retorts.

"Nope," Blaze growls and she deflates.

"I sleep with my knife and I'm taking this gun." She lowers her arm in defeat.

"Fine," Blaze nods. "You stay with Zander though." His hand lands on my shoulder and I groan.

"Fine," She shrugs, unaffected by the thought of sleeping in a room with me.

I mean why would she be affected? She's swallowing and fucking dick every day.

"Lucky cunt," Santos growls, and Darius shoots me a dirty look.

I lead her to a bedroom on the lower floor while the guys head upstairs.

"How will the interrogation start?" Her husky voice hits my back as we enter the room. "Orgasm deprivation? Knife play? Waterboarding?"

"The fuck?" I turn on her.

"I like most of those things, except waterboarding but I can hold my breath for a long ass time," she grins. "What's first?"

"First you can shower in there," I point to the bathroom and I open a drawer with some of my clothes. I have clothes at each of the guys' houses.

"Then you will sit in there while I wash this blood off me." I throw a t-shirt and a pair of boxers at her.

"Whatever," she huffs and turns on her heel into the washroom.

Is that blood on her thigh? I tip my head back on a groan and pray for my dick to deflate. I feel like I'm sixteen all over again.

I hear the shower start and then her voice floats out. She's fucking singing in the shower while washing blood off of herself, and she sounds like a dying cat.

What fucking gets me though is how she's so cool through all of this? Fuck it, the best way to corner someone is while they're naked, and I can get some images together for my spank bank.

I open the bathroom door and cringe when her voice gets louder, is she singing Adele? Dear fucking god she's singing Adele.

"I think you've broken every window in the fucking house." I growl, fighting hard to hold in my laugh.

"What's that?" She pokes her head out around the glass door. "Are you offering to wash my back?"

Fuck yes I am. I may be suspicious of the hooker, but I'm a fucking man, too. I drop my pants and whip off my shirt before climbing in behind her and shutting the door. I know I should be weary of her but I'm thinking with my fucking dick.

"No hidden knives in here, right?" I ask her and nearly shoot my load on her back when she grins over her shoulder.

She has a full back piece done and it's a detailed Grim Reaper. All black, blues, and purples swirling together and the gray of his scythe shines like it's actually catching the light's reflection. The art is so fucking detailed and beautiful. I look a little closer and notice it's not a male reaper but a female, one with strands of blonde hair blowing from under its hood.

"You'd be missing your balls if I did have a knife," she interrupts my gawking and looks down at my cock, then back up to my face. "Look who's bigger than Daddy."

That should turn me off, right? I shouldn't be harder because of it and I shouldn't be basking in praise that implies she's fucking my father.

"Unless you're going to put that mouth to good use, I suggest keeping it closed." I reach for the shampoo and my cock brushes her ass.

She tenses and then arches her back to press into me harder. I run my finger down her spine and revel in the moans that my touch brings out of her.

"You want my cock, Selene?" I ask. "After you just had Daddy dearest? I could smell you in my fucking house last night."

"Yes," she breathes. "I fucked your daddy last night, he even ate me out like a champ. The real question is, can you erase him? Are you better than him?"

Her words have me burning with anger and lust. I yank her around and lift her into my arms. This bitch has no idea what she just got herself into.

Chapter Fourteen

Selene

Zander's grip on my ass cheeks is bruising as he stalks out of the washroom, uncaring of the water being dropped everywhere. He throws me on the bed and in the next second he's hovering over me. His eyes are a mixture of green and brown, and right now they're looking at me in a silent challenge.

His upper body is completely tattooed and his legs each have a few here and there. His muscles flex as he holds himself above me and I grin at the scowl on his face. So much like Daddy indeed.

"After I fuck you," his hand curls around my chin painfully. "You no longer fuck my father."

"Are you asking me to quit my job?" I smirk.

"What?"

"I'm a prostitute." I roll my eyes, "and Daddy is a good client."

He rolls off me and sits at the edge of the bed. "Why are you fucking my father and how is it you can slam a blade into someone's head from across the room?"

"I fuck your father because he pays well." I sit up. "How close are you to him?"

"I hate him." His admission shocks me.

"Why?"

He looks at me over his shoulder and narrows his eyes.

"He killed my mother and he likes to abuse women." His brow raises. "He likes to rape women."

Huh. The shithead is telling me everything I already know but why? And a better question yet, what's his place in all of it?

"And you?" I lay back down, unashamed of my nakedness. "Do you help Daddy with all of that?"

"Me? I'm going to kill him." He snarls and grabs a pair of pants. "And if you happen to be there when I do, I'll kill you, too."

I want to tell him that I have the same plan, that I want to watch his fucking father die with his blood on my hands, and I want to help all the women he's enslaved. But I can't be sure he's telling me the truth.

I already knew about Henry killing his wife because I was there watching as he wrapped his hands around her throat and then threw her in the pool.

It was the final nail in the coffin and I made my decision to move forward on the plan to make Henry's death a long sufferable one.

Zander opens the bedroom door and slams it shut behind him. I have to find a way out of here tonight and I need to get away from this group of guys that both infuriate me and fucking have me dripping wet with only a few words.

I get out of the bed and pull my dress back on, then Zanders shirt over it. I slip the knife and gun back into my trench pockets and toss it on the bed.

I look behind me to the window that faces the street, do they really believe I wouldn't try to slip out? Or is that what they're hoping for?

I get up, pull on my trench, and thumb both the knife and gun in my pockets. Fuck it, I have never done what I've been told and I sure as fuck am not going to start now.

I pull the window up and look out with a laugh. It's about a five foot drop and I decide to hold my heels in my arms until after the jump. I can't afford a broken ankle right now.

I swing my leg over and then the other, sitting on the windowsill. I feel a twinge of guilt but swallow that fucker down quick, I don't owe these assholes a single thing, and I still don't know whose side they're on.

I hop out the window and land to the ground with a grunt. I slip on my heels and just walk myself away.

I got plans and there's no way in hell I'll be derailed by four hot men and their questionable loyalties.

Chapter Fifteen

Zander

"You let her get away?!" Darius yells into my empty bedroom.

"Nope." I say as I unlock my phone's screen.

"She's not here, asshole." Santos spreads his arms and turns on the spot.

"I know," I nod.

"He let my future wife get away." Santos sinks to the bed, "I had visions of Bonnie and Clyde."

"Will you shut up?" I snap at him.

"Where is she?" Blaze asks from over my shoulder.

"Three blocks down and just got in a vehicle." I answer him.

"What the fuck? You put a tracker on her phone?" Darius' grin takes over his whole face.

"Yeah," I smirk back at him, "just before I got in the shower with her."

His grin immediately falls and Santos jumps to his feet with a snarl, but Blaze grunts at me.

"Let's go follow this bitch and find out what she's all about," Blaze says then stalks towards the door.

"You two stay here," I point to Santos and Darius.

They each give me an eye roll but know it's the smart thing to do since the Diablos attacked us. It's been a while since they had the nerve to roll up on us and I think it has everything to do with my father. Maybe he's switching crews since our last argument.

We hop in Blaze's Camaro and death metal goth assaults my ears.

"I don't know how you listen to this shit," I say as I turn it down.

"Helps me concentrate," he replies.

I guide him to where the dot is moving on my screen and my

heart kicks up in speed. It's been a while since I've been on the hunt and I have to admit, it's one of my favorite things to do. I used to be so fucking good at it but then I realized I was hunting down girls for my father to rape and ship off as sex slaves.

"Just up here." I point to an apartment complex. "This is where she lives?"

Saying it's run down would be an understatement. The place has windows boarded and homeless sleeping out front. The bushes have begun to take over the walkway and started to grow their way up to the front door, which is hanging on by one hinge.

"Was that a rat?" Blaze asks as we see something the size of a cat scurry out.

"You stay with the car." I tell him because this car would be screaming to be stolen here. "I'll head in and see what's up."

I pull out my gun and hold it in my right hand as I get out of the car and make my way up the walkway. I enter the building and choke on a gag, covering my nose with my sleeve. It stinks of urine and maybe a rotting body somewhere.

The dot told me she was on the far right corner of the building and I am cursing myself for following her here. I could very well die from the stench alone, she can't possibly be living here, and if she is then she's not charging her clients near enough.

I walk down a short corridor and watch how each apartment becomes more and more decrepit. Doors hang off hinges showing rotting furniture and what could be blood stains on the floors. I get to the last one and the door is completely missing, the door jamb destroyed like someone kicked it down.

I creep inside and look around at the total destruction of the place. The couch is ripped apart and missing its cushions, there are dishes smashed all over the floor, and what looks to be a girl's barbie house is completely destroyed.

"I noticed the tracker when I got into the cab." Her voice hits my back and I turn to see her standing in the kitchen area, flipping her knife in the air. "Smart."

"What is this place?" I ask as I holster my gun.

"I grew up here," she nods to the Barbie house. "That was mine. My sister worked overtime for two weeks just so she could afford that for Christmas."

Alarm bells begin to ring but I step towards her, eager to hear more about her. I want to know why someone so beautiful and obviously tough ended up where she is.

"Our mother was a junkie and practically lived on the street. She only came back here when she remembered she had to eat. My sister Jan was six years older than me and by fourteen she had to drop out of school to raise me." She slams the knife's blade down into the counter. "That was the beginning of the end."

"What happened?" I ask, completely entranced.

"She got a few jobs and I would stay with the neighbors while she was out. Things were good until my mother started coming back around. She would beg Jan for money and when that wasn't enough, she began to pimp her daughters. I was ten years old when I had my first client."

The bile rushes up my fucking throat and I swallow several times to keep it from spewing.

"My sister had it worse, she was attractive and clearly becoming a curvy woman. The men loved her and my mother was making a killing. This went on for a few years and once I hit fifteen, my sister promised we were leaving. She had found an apartment for us and we were leaving the next night."

Her face hardens and she pulls the knife out of the counter and walks up to me.

"She left for work that night and I never saw her again. I hit the streets at fifteen and spoke to people, took some self-defense classes, and took up knife throwing classes. I found out a few months later that the word on the street was that my mother sold her to a man, a businessman who liked to deal in the flesh of young children."

My mouth goes dry and my limbs begin to tingle, I know where this is going.

"I confronted my mother and she fucking confessed to it, said my sister got her one thousand dollars. She was proud of herself and before she could finish her praise, I stabbed my knife through her eye. Right there on that couch, then I destroyed the place, and left, never to look back. But now I have a problem, Zander." Her chest hits mine and she stands toe to toe with me. "You're poking your nose in my business and I can't have you fuck up my plans."

"Was it my father?" I ask her, my eyes never leaving her big blues.

"He ended up with her and I can only imagine she had the same fate as your mother because otherwise she'd have come back to me by now."

"You want to kill my father," I nod, "looks like our plans match."

Her eyes narrow and she brings the point of her knife to my throat. I know she could kill me easily but I'm trusting the information I can provide would deter her.

"You're the Reaper Incarnate. Explains the tattoo on your back." I swallow and my skin presses further into the blade. "We can help you."

"How?" She growls. "How the fuck can I trust the son of that monster?"

"Because I'm a monster, too. And he needs to die for what he's done to my mother."

"I saw Darius and Santos at the last exchange, if we have the same plans why are you helping him *export*?"

"It's all a ruse so we can get more information and we always try to free as many as we can. Only problem is, I think he's onto us and he's the one that sent the Diablos last night. We needed another way in and I think you can help us with that."

I brush the hair out of her face and stare at her big blue eyes.

"Will you help us?" I ask her.

Chapter Sixteen

Selene

"**W**ill you help us?" Zander asks.

Will I? This has been my solo mission for so long and I'm having a hard time wanting to give it over to anyone else. Especially to the son of the man I plan on torturing for a while.

"I can see you fucking struggling to decide." He grabs my wrist that's holding the knife. "I don't expect you to trust me and I sure as fuck don't expect you to tell us the whole plan. But let us prove ourselves."

He needs an insider and I need information that he could provide. I drop the knife back to my side with a sigh.

"I need to know the shipments in advance and I need to know the process after the exchange." I tell him.

"I need you to worm your way into my father's bed and keep his attention. I want to know who calls him all hours of the night and where he goes at two or three in the morning." He counters.

"Probably prostitutes." I hold out my arms and gesture to myself.

"No," he shakes his head. "My father has his own whores. Which brings me back to how you got involved with him."

"Let's get out of here," I tell him and stride ahead of him out of the apartment that smells of piss and rot. "And you will never step foot where I live."

I turn on him, causing him to stop short and curse.

"If you try to track me again," I stand toe to toe with him. "I will cut your dick off and fuck you with it."

"I don't think that's physically possible..." He begins but I raise my brow at his protest. "Alright, no more trackers."

I exit the building as rats scurry down the steps, and see Blaze sitting in the vehicle. It's a fucking two-seater and I stop, looking back at Zander.

"Are you walking?" I smirk. "This neighborhood is a bit rough."

"Shut the fuck up," he grins back and steps around me.

He opens the door and sits in the seat, patting his lap. "Come sit on Daddy."

"I already sat on your daddy's face a few nights ago." I cross my arms.

Blaze barks out a deep thunderous laugh that shocks both me and Zander.

"Fuck, she's good," he continues to grin.

"Will you just get in here?" Zander growls.

I roll my eyes and sit on his lap. "Where are we going?"

"Back to the house, we have some questions for you." Blaze says as he pulls out onto the street.

Yeah, I got questions too, fuckers.

"Fuck yes!" Santos yells as we come in the door. "You got her!"

"You got me, fuckers." I turn and face Zander and Blaze, taking my knife out of my pocket and flipping it in my hand.

"Do we tie her down?" Darius asks, and I raise both eyebrows at Zander.

I turn around quickly and fling my knife, watching as it sails towards Darius' head. It nicks his cheek before continuing past and slamming into the plastered wall.

"I fucking dare you to try, bitch," I snarl.

Darius touches his cheek and looks at the blood on his hand with shock.

"I think I just came," Santos groans and drops down onto the couch.

Darius looks back at me and a crazy grin stretches across his face.

"We're gonna be the next Bonnie and Clyde." Santos moans.

Darius turns and pulls the knife out of the wall, tossing it back at me. I catch it and put it back in my trench pocket.

"We need to talk," Zander states and flings his arm over my shoulders.

I shrug off his arm and sit between Darius and Santos on the couch. I reach up and swipe the drop of blood gathering on Darius' cheek, popping my finger in my mouth. Zander gives me a pissed off look and Blaze looks just plain pissed off as they sit across from us.

"Selene here is the Reaper Incarnate," Zander tells the guys and the room falls deathly silent.

"No," Santos is the first to speak. "That's a dude. They found his latest victim in the alley yesterday and he was double her size."

I don't bother to fucking convince him otherwise because I really don't care what anyone believes.

"You're sitting beside the girl that took down the guy in the alley," Zander nods.

"I need to fuck that pussy so bad right now," Santos says into my ear, causing my pussy to throb at his words. My panties are fucking soaked.

"I may have to take you up on that offer," I say as I turn my head and our lips brush.

He's quick to grab the back of my neck and haul me up onto his lap. His lips crash into mine and his cock hardens between us. We're a moaning and writhing mess when I hear someone cursing.

"Can you separate the horny fucking teenagers?" Blaze growls. "We need to sort this shit out."

He's right, I know that, but Santos' dick is perfectly pressing against my panties underneath my dress and I give it one more slow grind.

"I'm fucking you after this," he says once our mouths separate. I can't complain about that idea.

He lifts me effortlessly, turning me to face the others but pulling my back against his front, keeping a firm grip on me as if I'm his personal possession. That should make me angry as fuck because I don't belong to anyone, but my head tilts back to rest on his shoulder and my nipples tighten instead.

Jesus fucking Christ, I hate girls who swoon over that kind of alpha bullshit, but here I am leaning into him with my pussy creaming for him.

Zander eyes us with irritation as he fills the guys in on our conversation from earlier, but Blaze flat out glares at me the whole time as if picturing his hands around my throat, choking the life out of me. I shiver, and Santos nips my neck hard, his warm breath teasing my skin as he whispers in my ear.

"Did you want me to fuck you to death right here? Because if you keep projecting your horny mood like that, you're going the right way about it," he warns, my breath hitching at the threat. I turn my head to reply, but Zander's voice cuts through the air sharply, stopping our banter.

"If you two can't focus on the conversation, I'll make you sit your ass on Blaze's lap. You want to know what we know, so do us all a favor and pay attention. I'm not going to fucking repeat myself."

Santos flips him the bird and runs a hand down my stomach, moving lower until he's cupping my pussy firmly.

"Don't tell me what to do with her, she's fucking mine. Besides, you just don't want me to fuck her right in front of you because you'll be the one getting distracted," he exclaims, letting out a snarl as Blaze stands and grabs my bicep, yanking me down beside him before I can even argue. He glares at me some more, his voice rough and full of venom.

"You can be a whore later, right now we need you to fucking focus. I'm doing you a favor, Santos will likely bleed you out in all his excitement."

I lean closer, brushing my lips against his cheek.

"God, I fucking hope so," then I drag the flat of my tongue up his cheek, giving him a wink. The best way to get to Blaze is to pretend I like him. Grumpy piece of shit.

He wipes his damp cheek with a scowl, but he doesn't say anything else as Zander draws our attention.

"Anyway, as I was fucking saying, we have many years' worth of shit against Henry. We have easily saved over one hundred girls, but so many more have been sold and lost. Like I said before, Selene, he's catching on to us, so we want to get this shit burned to the ground as soon as we can, before too many more girls get hurt. We have a shipment this week, so we need you to work on getting closer to him to try and distract him a little. I need to do some snooping in his office, but he's always in there when he's home. Do us a favor and try and occupy him elsewhere in the house. I have a feeling he's setting us up with the shipment, so I need to find out what the fuck he's planning. After the attack, I don't trust the bastard to play fair anymore," he explains, glancing at Darius who grunts.

"What if he fucking hurts her? We've all seen what the asshole is like with women. He could kill her."

"Like you're any better. Between you and Santos, do you have any idea how much damage you have done to all the sluts you've stuck your dicks in? Never mind, Selene can handle herself," Zander replies, his eyes sliding to mine as if challenging me to argue. I shrug, throwing a leg over Blaze's lap, ignoring the warning growl.

"I'll kill that fucker before he gets one over me, don't you worry about that, money bags."

"I'm worried that you will kill him. There's a reason he's still alive, idiot. He has a lot of reach in the underground because he spends so much money on skin, and he's helped move bodies for a long fucking time now. We need the intel on who else is involved, but we also need to play it smart so we don't get a big fat hit on our heads too. The only thing getting stabbed is your cunt with his dick, got it?" Zander snaps, my eyes narrowing as I shove myself up from the seat.

"Roger that, dick breath. Santos, care to join me? I feel like laying down and screaming for a while," I retort, Zander's eye twitching as Santos wastes no time throwing me over his shoulder with a psychotic laugh.

"I've got you, babe. Where do you want it? Wait, don't answer that. You don't get a say anyways. Darius, you coming?"

Darius stands, his tongue sweeping over his lips as a dark smirk takes over his face.

"Not yet, but I will be."

If they kept talking like that, I'm going to come in my panties before they even get their dicks out to play. If I'm able to walk tomorrow, I'm going to be highly disappointed.

Chapter Seventeen

Selene

Santos stalks up the hallway, laughing as I punch his firm ass cheek.

"I can walk, you know?" I growl, but Darius snorts from close behind us.

"Not for long, you little hell cat. Just shut up and take it."

"Keep that kind of talk up, and I'll come before we even get to where we're going," I coo, letting out a breathy moan as Santos' large hand cracks against my butt sharply.

"You don't know what you're in for by taunting us, you cheeky wench."

We enter a room and I'm thrown down on a bed, my body bouncing slightly from the impact. Santos yanks Zander's shirt off me, and I move to sit up but he presses a hand against my shoulder, pinning me down as he pulls a knife from his pocket, his eyes twinkling with craziness and desire.

"Don't fucking move," he warns before grabbing the material of the dress and slicing down the front of it with the blade, ripping it completely open to expose my bra and panties.

"Hey! That was fucking expensive!" I snap, but he raises an eyebrow, gliding the blunt end of the cool blade from my throat to my stomach.

"I'll get you a new one. I wasn't kidding when I said you don't get a say, this is our show, not yours," he states in a dark voice, my skin shivering as he slips the blade under the material of my panties, giving it a slight tug to tear it as well.

He doesn't give me time to argue before slamming his lips down on mine, tossing his blade aside to fist my hair tightly. I moan, arching my body up to try and grind against him, but he keeps his body away from my touch, proving he's in charge.

The sound of clothes dropping to the floor catches my attention, and I gasp as Santos slips his hand between my legs, slicking his fingers with my creamy juices before shoving two fingers inside me roughly without warning.

I groan loudly into his mouth, my hands gripping his shoulders as if to push him away, but I dig my nails in to keep him close. A feral growl rips from him at my approval as he moves his face back to stare down at me, his fingers moving faster and deeper.

Fingers wrap around my wrists and pull my hands away from Santos, a deep chuckle coming from Darius as he pulls my arms back above my head. I glance up to see him butt naked, a thick rope clasped between his teeth.

For a moment I tense, not wanting to give them the ability to trap me, but I relax slightly as Santos runs his nose down my throat, nipping at my skin.

"We're going to fuck you so hard that the only words you'll be able to remember are our names. Heads up, you don't get a safe word," he murmurs against my soft skin, a breathy moan leaving me.

They are scrambling my fucking brain already. Allowing them to tie me up is a stupid move, but I am beyond caring at this point.

The rough rope wraps around my wrists, and Darius grins down at me once I'm secured to the headboard and I give it a test tug. It isn't going to come loose any time soon.

"You won't get out of that until I let you, but it's cute that you tried. Don't struggle, or you'll get some wicked rope burn," he warns, vanishing from my sight for a second, but I soon feel rope on my ankles as he ties my feet to the foot of the bed, spreading me out for their taking.

"Do you really believe I'll run off in the middle of sex?" I scoff with amusement, but Darius just stands beside the bed, continuing to grin.

"Not sure yet, but I've tied you down for two reasons. Nothing gets my dick harder than seeing my ropes restraining someone, and Santos is likely to make you jump all over the place the moment his face is between your sinful legs."

I don't have to wonder why for very long, because Santos scoots his body down the bed and nips my clit almost painfully, causing my hips to lift slightly from the bed as a shriek of surprise leaves me. He smirks up at me as I strain my neck to glare down at him, and his tongue darts out to lick right up my slit.

I drop my head back to the pillow with a groan.

"Selene, keep your fucking eyes on Santos, or you'll be punished," Darius threatens, and I do my best to keep my eyes on the wicked man between my legs as he licks and sucks at my pussy like a man starved.

My body's a shaking mess, and I drop my head back slightly without thinking, a sharp sting piercing my side.

I whip my head up to see Santos blade against my skin, a wicked glint in his eye as he digs the blade in slightly as I glare at him.

A drop of blood trickles down my skin, and he pulls back to watch it. His breath fans across my damp folds and I whimper at the loss of contact, but my pussy clenches as he leans over me, keeping his eyes on mine and he runs his tongue across the small amount of blood.

I pull against the ropes and growl, hating not having my hands free.

"Untie me so I can touch you," I demand, but he smirks, cocking his head to the side as he sits back.

"Why the fuck would I do that when I'm having so much fun watching you squirm?" He asks, but Darius blocks my sight from him as he sits his bare ass on my chest, fisting his hard length and running the tip across my lips.

"You talk too much. Open wide, Reaper," he orders, making me scowl for a moment at the use of my name before doing as he asks.

He's not gentle as his fingers tangle in my hair to tug me over his dick more, a groan leaving him as I take him deep, despite the awkward angle.

"That's better, choke on my dick," he mutters, lifting himself a fraction to force himself deeper.

I choke, a sadistic grin taking over his face as he pushes down my throat even more, forcing saliva to slip from my lips and down my chin. I've spent my life chasing down guys like this, letting them treat me like dirt until I get the last laugh, but something tells me these guys won't humiliate me. Hurt me, maybe, but not humiliate me.

"Fuck, you love choking on it, don't you? Darius, she's wet as fuck," Santos groans almost as if in pain, bending down to suck on my clit, going back to stroking his fingers in and out of my now drenched pussy.

He finds that magic spot inside me and sucks harder on my bundle of nerves, causing my body to lock up as my orgasm rips through me. I swear my eyes roll into my fucking head as he keeps the same pace.

Chapter Eighteen

Zander

J walk into the bedroom just as Selene comes, her body writhing under Darius who's fucking her mouth like a mad man. I have to admit, she doesn't scare easily. He's being rough as fuck, and I almost cum in my fucking boxers at the sight.

Santos sits back with a grin, licking his lips before wiping his mouth with the back of his hand.

Selene's eyes flutter as she glances over at me in her orgasmic haze, a small smile tugging at her lips as Darius climbs off her.

"You coming to join us, money bags? Plenty of room," she giggles, causing my dick to jerk to life. I am supposed to get her the fuck away from them, but she looks fucking stunning laid out on the bed at their mercy.

I can't even form words, but Santos goes ahead and snaps me out of it.

"If you're going to stand there like a little bitch, at least open your mouth and swallow my load like one."

I glare at him, but Selene tugs against her restraints, watching me with pleading blue eyes. She wants me, and my dick is one hundred percent on board with that plan, but I'm not going to take her with these two fuckers. I want her in my bed, screaming my fucking name, not theirs.

I pull all my willpower together and take a step back, giving them a dirty look.

"Nope. Have a good night," I bite out, stalking from the room before I can change my mind.

Blaze raises an eyebrow as I enter the kitchen, amusement hidden deep inside.

"Something wrong, brother?" He questions, and I grit my teeth with annoyance.

"I'm fucking fine."

I don't know why I snapped at the others, and now I'm taking my mood out on Blaze. Fuck, I do know. I have a thing for the hooker who's fucking my piece of shit father.

"You should've hauled her out of there if you want her so bad," Blaze says, ignoring my attitude.

"Am I that fucked up?" I ask him as I sit at the table. "I want the whore my father is using as a cum dumpster."

"Yeah," he shrugs. "But being fucked up is our thing. Just tell her you get her next."

"What?" I chuckle at him. "We're all just going to have her, like a big happy sharing family?"

"Don't bring me into this bullshit," he snarls. "I don't want the dirty whore."

"Alright, my bad," I chuckle and back out of the kitchen. "Let's get a hold of Mack and find out when he's setting up his meat delivery to my father."

"Yeah, we'll call him after I get some sleep."

Blaze runs cold until he's triggered and then the mean fucker is scalding fucking hot. Don't fuck with what's his or he will blast a bullet into your brain in a matter of seconds. He's guarded and doesn't trust easily and having Selene in on our plans is most likely starting to trigger him.

He doesn't trust her and I don't blame him, we don't know her but I saw her inside that fucking apartment. She showed me a piece of herself and I believed every word she said. I really do believe her mother sold her sister and I also believe my father ended up owning her. I want to find out more and the only way I can do that is if Selene can distract my father.

My father keeps everything locked up in that office and it's well secured with video surveillance. But I can drop the feed and loop it for ten minutes, all I'll need is ten fucking minutes in that office.

I just need her help.

Having him watch me as I came all over Santos' face made my orgasm that much better. I fucking want him to come back and join in with us because the more dicks, the better. I feel a quick swipe of the blade against my inner thigh and then my blood once again rolling towards the bed.

I growl as I look down and see Darius coating his finger in the blood while Santos licks it off the tip of the blade. Then Darius slips that bloody finger inside me and I whimper at the sweet intrusion.

"Start fucking her," Santos says as he gets up and comes to the head of the bed. "Now it's time to choke on my cock, Reaper."

I grin at him and snap my teeth towards his tip.

"Don't get crazy," he grins right back. "I'll fuck you with my knife instead."

Darius presses his cock to my entrance and I gasp as he begins to stretch me wide. He takes his time for the first few inches and I lift my head to get a better look. It's when he looks up to me with a crazy laugh that I begin to fucking worry.

He slams home and I scream through the pleasurable pain.

"Keep that mouth open wide," Santos chuckles and his cock thrusts into my mouth, hitting the back of my throat. "Gag all over my cock."

I do, I gag all over his cock and his sinister laugh sounds when saliva drips down my chin. Darius picks up the pace between my legs making me meet Santos' thrusts and forcing him further down my throat.

Then Santos crams himself in further and my throat constricts around his length as I struggle to fucking breathe.

"Fuck yes," Darius groans. "She's tightening up, keep that throat filled."

I pull against my binds as I attempt to dislodge Santos from my airway, and my wrists sting with the burn from the harsh rope.

"Told ya not to fight against those." Darius slams in one more time and I feel his hot cum shoot inside of me.

Santos pulls out in time with Darius and I suck in air, choking as my tight chest begins to loosen.

"You crazy motherfuckers," I growl at them, and Santos is once again between my legs.

"I want to taste my boy inside of you." That's the only warning I get as his mouth begins sucking at my pussyhole.

"Fuck," I exclaim as his tongue slides inside of me, licking me thoroughly.

It's fucking turning me on that he's sucking and licking his friend's cum from inside of me, and I feel myself coiling tighter again.

He gets up and lines himself up with my entrance, thrusting into me with a powerful plunge. My pussy clamps down on him and I scream as he grabs my waist and fucks me into oblivion. I crest the high of my orgasm and fall over the edge, screaming things completely unintelligible. I don't give a fuck though because I am having an out of body experience.

Santos bottoms out inside me a few moments later, groaning through his release, and I feel Darius undoing the restraints on my wrists.

I'm out of it, completely fucking destroyed, and the last thing I remember is someone washing my pussy with a warm cloth.

Chapter Nineteen

Zander

When I finally wake up, it's late afternoon and I growl that I've missed half the day. I get out of bed and shower, finally pounding one out to the image of her blue eyes as she came.

I get to the kitchen and almost cum again when I smell the coffee and bacon. I walk in and find Selene at the stove with just my t-shirt on, her long tanned legs on display as she cooks the bacon.

Darius chuckles when he sees me gawking.

"She's a fucking sex maniac," he tells me as Selene turns to look at me.

"Good morning." Her voice is so fucking sexy and husky.

"Morning." I mumble and head for the coffee machine.

I don't want to look at her standing there looking satisfied in my shirt when I attributed nothing to that state, and the sight of the small cuts on her neck has me boiling inside. Santos really laid into her, and Darius too if the rope burns around her wrists mean anything.

"Your daddy has called and summoned me to your big ole house," she says, her words laced heavy with sarcasm. "Bet he misses this pussy."

"He'd be fucking stupid not to," Darius chuckles and gets up to leave the kitchen.

The anger that comes over me at her words is fucking swift, and I grab her blonde hair in my hand and haul her over to face me.

"Do you think I need to hear about some whore fucking my father?" I snarl into her face, my spit hitting her cheeks.

"Why are you so pissed if I'm just a whore?" She's calm, unfussed by my violent outburst. Like she knows she can take me on.

The thought has me rock hard in my pants and I drag her in closer, pressing into her stomach.

"Because you've ridden almost every dick but mine." I'm shocked at my admission.

"All you have to do is ask," she purrs up at me and I release my hold on her hair.

"Whatever." I turn my back and take a few deep breaths. "What time are you going there?"

"Same time as before. Midnight," she answers and begins to hum as she cooks.

I can't be in this room with her right now while she's looking thoroughly fucked, because my cock has ideas and I can't seem to get a grip on my sanity with her around.

"Get dressed and let's plan this shit out," I grumble.

"I have no clothes because your psycho friend decided it would be fucking fun to cut them off me."

Fucking Santos.

"I'll grab you some pants." I'm out of the kitchen and the air feels clearer, not so cloyed with her scent.

It's no better seeing her in my shirt and pants as she moans over bacon, sucking the grease off her fingertips. All of us - even Blaze - are squirming in our fucking seats and refusing to look away. She eats like she's perpetually stoned, enjoying every fucking morsel.

"I need to fill your mouth again," Darius groans, and I watch as he grabs onto his cock.

"Same," Santos moans.

"Fuck off," Blaze growls and slams his fist onto the table. "These women, these *children*, need our help and instead of making a plan, you're lusting after a fucking hooker."

The room falls silent and I can feel the tension thicken.

"That's not very nice, scary man," Selene says, popping her fingers out of her mouth. "I have my plan and I've had it for a long fucking time."

"So have we," I tell her, "but if we're going to work together, we need those plans to mesh."

"Alright," she drops the bacon to her plate. "I am going to your father's place tonight. I plan on letting him do dirty nasty things to me and that's where you come in. Get in that office and check behind the painting of his father."

It's like being hit by a fucking freight train. I've been looking for his vault for years and I narrowed it down to his office, I just didn't know where inside.

"How do you know that?" I ask.

"The last time I was there, he fucked me in the office, and I saw the painting. It was slightly off center which could happen, but it was the dust free bottom right corner that really caught my eye. Like someone keeps touching it on that exact spot, several times a day."

Fuck, she's good. I can feel my impression of her shifting in this exact moment and it's fucking shocking. Sure, I knew she could maim, fucking kill, and I knew she used her pussy as a weapon as well, but she was also fucking smart.

She just shaved off all the time it would take me to find the fucking vault in his office. I wouldn't even need the full ten minutes now.

My heart begins to race with excitement and before I can even fucking stop it, I'm launching myself around the table and crashing my mouth into hers. She tastes of salty bacon and something else entirely unique to her.

My tongue pushes itself into her mouth and she's moaning, clutching to the front of my shirt. I hear the clearing of a throat and finally snap out of my stupor, instantly pulling away from her mouth.

"Well," she runs a finger across her swollen red lips. "Three down."

"That's all you'll get," Blaze says, his voice dark and mean.

"Sure," she shrugs and starts back into her bacon. "So, good plan?"

"Yes." I sit back in my chair.

"Cool." She sticks out her hand, "someone pay me for the dress that Slasher over here destroyed. I need to impress big dick daddy."

And she's back to her-fucking-self.

REAPED

THE REAPER INCARNATE

Chapter Twenty

Selene

Santos handed me a credit card and told me there's no limit. Motherfucker has shit for brains because I just bought myself a new wardrobe and enough alcohol to drown myself and then some. I bought Louboutin's too because why not? Daddy Henry needs to be impressed.

I stand at the mirror, checking myself out at every angle, and decide I'm a hot bitch. This tight black tube dress is clinging to every curve, making my tits pop, and my ass ripe. I'm sure Henry will love all the easy access to my best parts.

I get a text from Zander telling me everything is in place and now I just need to wait for Henry to tell me where to meet his driver. About twenty minutes later, Henry sends me a text to meet the driver in the same location as last time.

I get to the Rolls Royce and it's the same driver, only this time the fucker is a bit more curious. He keeps looking at me through the rear-view mirror and it's making me want to shoot the fucker in the back of the head.

We finally pull up to the house and when he comes around to open my door, he has the audacity to ask for my number. But being the good hooker that I am, I give him the local pizza joint's number by my house and blow him a kiss for good measure.

Henry meets me just inside the door and his eyes rake over me appreciatively.

"Good week?" The piece of shit asks.

"Yes," I smile at him. "I expect to be paid tonight for the last time as well." I wink at him.

"Yes, of course," he nods and heads for the office.

"Wait," I call out to him. "Can we go somewhere else?"

I keep to the script that Zander and I rehearsed.

"Pardon?" He quirks his brow.

"This is such a big house," I widen my eyes. "Do you blame me for wanting to see it?"

He relaxes and throws me a smile. "What would you like to see?"

"I have a thing for cars and I've always wanted to be fucked on the hood of a classic."

He tips his head back and laughs. "What makes you think I have any classics?"

"Any car over a hundred grand will do." I flutter my lashes and he laughs again.

"I will admit, it sounds intriguing." He takes my hand and leads me away from the office. I know the layout and I grin to myself when we head for the garage.

According to Zander, it's soundproofed and the furthest point in the house from the office.

The second we step into the garage, my breath leaves me in a rush. There's about ten cars in here and each one of them is at least a hundred grand.

"Wow," I say and for the first time tonight, I'm not acting.

"Pick your poison," he offers and gives me a wink.

It's fucking unfortunate that Henry is a slimy motherfucker that's into raping girls and if he doesn't end up killing them, he sells them to the highest bidder, because this piece of shit is handsome.

I walk over to a red Corvette and run my hands along the hood.

"That's one of my son's," He says.

"Oh?" I look over my shoulder at him. "Think he'll mind?"

I begin to pull up the hem of my skirt, planting my feet apart, and bend over to rest my elbows on the hood, my ass out and waiting for him.

He comes up behind me, running his hands along my ass cheeks, and then up my back to settle against my neck.

"All these cuts and bruises." His voice is quiet.

"Some clients get a little rough," I shrug and look back at him.

"And you allow that?" He asks, sounding curious.

"If the pay is right."

His hand brushes along the top of my head and before I know it, he slams my face down onto the hard, cold surface of the hood. I grunt at the impact and count to ten to stop myself from attacking him back.

I need him to believe I'm nothing more than a helpless whore. But it's fucking hard.

"Now we can really have fun." His chuckle is dark and foreboding.

I hear his belt come undone and I stay completely still under his firm hand. I could easily get out of this and kill the fucker with my bare hands, but I'm sadistic and like my sex just as sadistic.

He releases my head and I lift it to look behind me, only to have his belt slipped over my head and around my neck. This is a little disconcerting, especially knowing he likes to strangle and kill girls.

The belt tightens and breathing becomes difficult. I feel his fingers brush my core and I can't help as it clenches in anticipation. Greedy little bitch.

He rips my thong off and I hiss at the sting, his laugh grinding my fucking nerves.

But my pussy is wet, like I said, sadistic.

I hear the crinkle of a condom wrapper and the belt tightens again as he lines himself up. I may die here tonight but at least my pussy will be thoroughly beaten.

I plant my hands and brace myself for what I know will be a rough fucking ride. He doesn't let me down as he props my knee to the hood and roughly plunges inside me. My mouth falls open at the intrusion as my pussy grips his length.

"Fuck," he groans as he pulls on the belt and slides all the way out.

When he slams back in, my hands jerk off the hood and I strain against the belt, choking for a split second until I get my hands back under me. The heightened sensation from being choked and fucked hard, has me climbing towards my release.

Just as I'm about to fucking crash over the edge I hear his voice.

"This looks interesting."

Motherfucker. This just *got* interesting. Henry's thrusts falter as his son's voice echoes around us.

"Did it have to be on my car?" He sounds slightly amused.

The belt around my neck loosens and I greedily suck in a lung full of air.

"Don't stop on my account," Zander purrs out as he goes to the driver's side door and leans against the top. "She's not your usual."

Henry is still inside of me and I can feel his cock twitch but he still hasn't said anything. I give Zander a look that says *what the fuck are you doing?*

Henry begins to slowly pump back into me and I moan as Zander keeps his eyes on my face. It's fucking hot because I'm between a father and son. Henry slams into me and I gasp as he tightens the belt back around my throat.

Zander reaches out and brushes the hair from my face.

"How is her cock sucking?" He asks his father.

At his words, my stomach tightens and I moan as I feel myself cresting again.

"She's good," Henry grunts behind me, and I can't help but grin at Zander. His daddy thinks I suck cock well.

He sees my smug look and his eyes narrow as he begins to undo the button and zipper on his pants. Is he going to join in?

The belt tightens and Henry's voice drifts from behind me.

"Be a good little whore and suck his dick too."

Zander has his cock in his hand and I can't help but wonder if the two of them have done this before. I open my mouth and run my tongue along his tip, tasting him.

Then Zander grabs my hair and forces my head back to stick his cock in my mouth. The belt tightens to hold me in place as Zander brutally fucks my mouth and breathing is not an option.

"Dirty fucking whore," Henry's hand slaps down on my ass. "You'd choke on any cock, wouldn't you?"

I can feel the tears slip down my cheeks from lack of oxygen and my pussy is leaking just as much from Henry's punishing rhythm. He slaps down on my ass again and I groan around Zander's cock in my mouth.

Zander pulls out of my mouth, giving me just enough time to take a breath, and then he's ploughing back in. The ferociousness from both father and son have me tumbling over the edge, my vision blacking out.

"She's so fucking tight around my cock." Henry slams in once more and releases inside of me.

"Her mouth is like heaven," Zander moans and shoots his load down my throat.

The belt comes off my neck and I fall forward onto the hood of the car, still swallowing down Zander's bitter cum. I hear them both doing up their pants and then a large wad of bills lands beside my face.

"She's expensive," Zander whistles.

"I owed her for another night. Mind walking her out? I need to get work done." I lean up in time to watch Henry walk away and back into the house.

I grab up the bills and whistle to myself when I see at least five thousand dollars.

"Did you get it?" I ask him.

"Yeah," he heads to the driver's side door. "We need to leave before he notices it missing."

I'm sore between my legs after my night with Santos and Darius, and now Henry. So, walking to the passenger side is difficult.

But I just had a Daddy and Son sandwich, the fucking pain is worth it.

THE REAPER INCARNATE

Chapter Twenty-One

Zander

Holy fucking shit. Quite sure that was the best head I'd ever had in my goddamn life. If Selene wasn't already consuming my senses, she sure as fuck is now.

I glance over at her as we pull up in the driveway at Santos' place, noticing her staring out the window blankly.

"Were we too rough with you?" I ask as I kill the engine and unbuckle my belt, but she snorts and glares at me with complete defiance in her stunning blue eyes, almost taking my breath away.

"That was nothing. I can take more than a belt and a rich dude sandwich. Pretty sure I'd scare Santos if I let loose completely," she huffs, causing my lips to kick up into a smirk.

I startle her slightly as I grab her chin roughly and kiss her hard, sitting back after a second to stare into her eyes.

"Next time, it's going to be my dick in your cunt, not Henry's. I'm going to fuck you so hard that all memories of that asshole will be erased from your fucking head, and my dick's all you can think about," I say in a low voice, her body shivering at my words.

We climb from the car and head towards the house, nearly getting bowled over by Santos and Darius who seemed to think they'd never see her again.

"You're back! How was the old dude dick? Actually, don't answer that or I'll go over there and gut him for touching you," Santos scowls, hauling her against him roughly and hugging her so tight that she chokes slightly.

"Santos, I need air," she manages to get out, making him laugh as he steps back and ruffles her wavy blonde hair, much to her annoyance.

"No you don't, you held your breath longer than that when Darius' dick was jammed down your throat. So, you two were successful?" He asked, his gaze bouncing between us.

"Took two seconds. Selene knew where the safe was hidden," I smirk, but she just shoots me a fake sweet smile, fluttering her long lashes at me.

"Thank fuck, or you would have missed out on dumping your load in me."

Blaze looks at me as if I were slacking on the job, but Darius grins.

"You got to tap that, huh? If it were possible after what we did to her, and then Henry, I'd say you definitely have a pin dick and no cunt skills whatsoever," he teases, but Selene just can't help herself as she rubs against me, her voice sultry.

"Oh, he just shut me up while Daddy dearest filled my cunt. You taste good, Zander," she breathes, standing on tiptoe to lick me up the side of my face. She is lucky I don't get Santos to hold her down while I fuck her, sore pussy be damned.

Blaze manages to look surprised, but Santos cackles with laughter, his psychotic hooting bouncing off the walls.

"You joined in with Henry? You sick fuck, I love you. I say you and I fuck her senseless, and I accidently slip one in you, just to see how freaky you get!" He laughs, sitting on the couch and motioning for Selene to join him.

My body becomes cold as she moves away from me and lowers herself onto Santos lap, snuggling against his chest.

"It's not even that freaky. It's not like he rubbed balls with his dad," she sighs, bored of the conversation.

"Did you even get what you went there for?" Blaze snaps, anger and irritation seeping out of him in waves.

He stalks towards me and snatches the papers that poke out from my pocket, running his eyes over them without waiting for my answer.

Darius rolls his eyes and plonks his ass down beside Santos, pulling Selene's feet onto his lap and absently massaging them.

"Anything weird stick out to you? Assassination plans or some shit?" He asks, tilting his chin at me to answer him. I shrug, feeling Blaze's annoyance from beside me without turning my head.

"I glanced over things quickly, I didn't read in detail."

"That's because you were too busy dicking daddy's whore," Blaze grunts, not taking his eyes off the paperwork.

Santos scowls, and I really think he's about to go kill Henry and fuck up our plans, but Selene stands and moves up to Blaze, dipping her fingers below the elastic on his sweats and leaning forward with a coy smile.

"Sounds like someone's jealous. You want some release, grumpy? I'll even give you a freebie because I'm a good buddy like that."

His hand darts up, his fingers spanning around her pretty neck as he squeezes firmly, swatting her other hand away from his pants.

"Do not fucking touch me," he grits out, but she's not even fucking fazed as her eyes fill with some form of crazy lust, my dick jerking slightly.

"If you're going to choke me, at least do it from behind. I bet you're a savage in bed. Can you tear the pussy up, Blaze?" She breathes, causing Santos and Darius to groan.

Blaze glares at her for a split second before shoving her back and slamming the papers against my chest.

"You go over this shit, I'm leaving. Control your bitch before I have to," he spits before stalking from the house and slamming the door behind him.

Selene pouts, and I can't help myself as I wrap her hair around my fist and tug her flush with my front, dipping down to suck her pouty lip between my teeth. She stares at me with heated eyes, but I chuckle and nip her sharply before letting her go.

"You need to sleep. I'll give these papers a once over and we can talk about it in the morning. It's late, and you've had a workout today."

Santos goes to stand but I put my hand out, stopping his escape.

"You two on the other hand can sit here with me and leave her the fuck alone. Her pussy won't vanish overnight, so let her rest."

"Fucking seriously?" Santos snaps, but Darius rolls his eyes, not bothering to move.

"Santos, let her sleep. We can fuck her cunt in half tomorrow."

Always the problem solver.

Santos perks up at that idea, letting Selene head to bed without argument.

I am actually surprised when she doesn't argue, but I can tell she's sore. She's been walking funny ever since we got back to my place.

Once she is out of the room, I hand the papers to Darius to glance over, and I sit beside them to look over things.

All I know is my father sure as shit has caught onto us, because one of the papers is a letter from some cunt, letting him know he'd accepted the job and it is none other than the leader of the Diablos, Antonio.

Now that we know who the fuck is on our asses, it's time to start planning on how to burn Henry's kingdom to the fucking ground.

I usually would have beat Zander's balls for dismissing me to bed, but I can't lie, my coochie hurts and I am tired as fuck. I'll let them find the information that we need, then hopefully by the time I wake up we can get a plan into order.

I feel the bed dip, just a slight movement behind me as I lie in bed, I instinctively feel for my knife under the pillow and quickly turn, straddling the person to pin them to the mattress with my knife against their throat.

Santos' eyes fill with desire as he thrusts up against me, his voice rough from sleep.

"Wow, you like to get into it early, huh baby? Alright, but just a quickie or we'll get in trouble from the cock blocking assholes," he grins like the crazy fucker he is, and I press the blade more firmly against his skin as I lean down to speak in his ear.

"That depends. Do I get to tie you up this time?" I whisper, his dick jerking from under me.

"Maybe later, kitten. Right now I need you to get on your back and spread those legs for me. Keep the knife out though, I like it," he purrs, sliding his hand up my waist and along my smooth skin. A quickie couldn't hurt.

I pull the knife back and climb off him, giggling as he rolls me onto my stomach and pins my arms against my back, holding my knife between his teeth with a chuckle. He tugs my panties down my legs and lifts my ass in the air, dropping my knife onto the bed so he can open a condom without letting my hands go with the other.

He slams into me, causing me to scream into the pillows as my pussy adjusts to the sudden intrusion, his fist going to my hair to yank my face away from the pillow clouds.

"Scream my name. Let's see if we can both cum before they kick the door down," he growls, and my pussy clenches in excitement at that idea. I arch my back as I feel the cool handle of my blade press against my clit, and I moan loudly as he starts rubbing it against my sensitive bundle of nerves while pounding into me.

He slows, bringing his free hand around in front of my face and running his thumb along my lips.

"Suck it," he demands, a groan of satisfaction coming from him as I draw it into the wet heat of my mouth and roll my tongue around it until he pulls it away from me.

He runs his hand down my spine, hooking his wet thumb into my ass and picking up the pace again, the blade handle moving faster.

"Fuck, fuck, fuck, I'm going to cum!" I blurt out, and he presses his thumb deeper into my ass, causing me to explode. White light flashes behind my eyelids as I scream, his thrusts becoming erratic as he tosses the knife aside and grabs hold of my waist, rutting into me so hard that my orgasmic stars get fucking stars.

The door slams open and bounces off the wall just as Santos comes hard, shoving into me as deeply as possible with a grunt. He drops beside me, his eyes lighting up as he stares at my naked body.

"Fuck, that's so hot," he exclaims, causing me to look over my shoulder to see bloodied handprints on my waist. I frown in confusion, but Santos laughs like a psycho, holding his bloodied hand in front of himself.

"Well shit, maybe I held the knife a little too tightly. Whoops! You look hot as fuck with my blood on you, Selene. Pretty sure it's going to make me cum again."

Blaze is in the doorway, the rage on his face slipping slightly as he stares right at my pussy that's still in the air. I wiggle my ass, snapping him out of it as I giggle.

"You want a go? Might make you smile for once in your fucking life, angry man," I taunt, not at all surprised when he sneers at me and gets hold of his wandering thoughts.

"Santos, get down to the kitchen and help Zander. You were supposed to leave her to sleep, not come in here and have play time," he grumbles, his eyes narrowing on me as I roll onto my back and spread my legs, running a hand down my mound to tease my clit.

"You sure you don't want to start your day with a smile? I think it would be good for you."

He barks at Santos to hurry the fuck up before storming off, leaving Santos with me unsupervised. I waggle my eyebrows at him but he groans and rolls off the bed, putting distance between us as he throws the condom in the bin by the bathroom door.

"You heard the grumpy bastard, playtime is over. We will get back to this later, you little minx. I'm going to get Darius to tie you up again and I'm going to choke you with my dick until you pass the fuck out. Hopefully, Zander will want to come play too, then we could fill all three holes at once. Fuck, I'm getting hard again just thinking about it. I'm going to go and do some work before Zander stalks up here and shouts like a jealous idiot. Maybe blow him again before we get into this plan, might relax him a little," he jokes before leaving the room to give me some peace.

I wince as I sit up, making my way into the bathroom to wash up, having to rummage through the drawers for something fresh to wear.

Fairly sure Zander's eyes nearly fall out of his head when he sees me wander into the kitchen in his clothes again.

Blaze huffs as if I'm the reason nothing's getting done, but Zander finally snaps out of his staring and clears his throat, motioning to Darius.

"You and Santos are scoping out one of Henry's shipments today, Blaze is talking to some contacts about the assholes Henry sent after us, and I have to get our security bumped up in case of another attack. Selene, you…"

"I'm busy," I cut in, all their eyes swinging to me.

"Pardon?" Zander snorts, "Doing what exactly? Thought you wanted to fucking help?"

"I do, but Daddy Walton isn't my only client that I have to deal with. I have another piece of shit to take out today, but then I can be back here tonight if you need me," I explain, giving them a half shrug. Blaze looks ready to kill me, but Zander seems almost relieved.

"Alright, you handle that, and we will handle this shit. Let us know if you need back up," he offers, earning a snort from me.

"There's more chance of you needing to call me for back up, money bags, but thanks for the offer."

Santos grins at me like I'm the best thing he's ever seen, and Darius chuckles, handing me a coffee with a wink.

"I'll need help getting off this afternoon, so I'll definitely be calling you in for back up."

I can't even be mad, because hello, coffee?

I sip it with a groan, all four sets of eyes watching me with the same intensity as if I'd taken my fucking clothes off and shaken my tits at them. I quirk an eyebrow at Darius, biting my lip before speaking softly.

"How many freebies do you think you're getting, exactly?"

"You're not even a real hooker," he pouts, his eyes lighting up as I move towards him and kiss his cheek.

"The money doesn't hurt though. My funds will run out eventually and I'll have to move on again," I reply, Santos' head whipping around to glare at me.

"What the fuck are you talking about? You're not going anywhere, you're fucking mine, Selene. If you leave, I'll fucking drag you back by your hair!" He snaps, and I struggle not to giggle as his eye twitches.

"You can only kill so many assholes before moving on. I don't want to get caught, and my list of people is practically worldwide. Doling out punishments is hard work, but someone's gotta do it," I shrug, but his eyes are blazing as he grabs my bicep, sloshing my coffee over the brim of the cup.

"You're. Not. Leaving. Me."

Darius doesn't look happy with me either, but he gets between us and manages to get Santos to release his hold on me.

"C'mon, we all have shit to do today. We can get on with our shit, and she'll meet us back here later. Won't you, Selene?" He says firmly, waiting for me to nod before letting his friend go. Santos scowls and stalks off with Darius behind him, slamming the front door as he leaves, but Blaze just snorts.

"Knew your pussy was going to cause fucking problems. Do us a favour and get this shit done so you can fuck off. I'll see you later, Zan," he grunts and takes off too, leaving Zander and I alone. Zander rubs his temples before looking my way, with conflict in his gaze.

"I really wish you two would get along," he mutters with irritation.

Why the fuck does he care if we get along or not? Didn't I just say I was leaving? Maybe he's not the brightest crayon in the fucking box?

"Hey, all he's gotta do is bend me over this kitchen table and I'll be his best friend. He's the one with the issue, not me. I'm going to go and get ready for my date. I want to go dress shopping with the money Henry gave me," I grin, but he rolls his eyes and thrusts his credit card at me.

"Save your money. Take this and buy a new outfit. Don't wreck it while you're annihilating old rich assholes today. I want to tear it from you myself when you get back here," he says in a low voice.

My coochie clenches in anticipation with that plan, so I smirk and kiss his cheek, making sure to brush my body against his.

"Sounds good, Zan. I'll see you later," then I call an Uber and head off home to get some of my plans together for the day.

Chapter Twenty-Two

Selene

Zander is going to cum down his fucking leg when he sees this dress on me. It is bright red, strapless, and it practically stays up with willpower and prayers. It is tight as fuck, and I love how good my ass looks in it.

My next victim, Harold Aster, is in his early sixties. He's done well to cover his tracks, but not well enough to hide from me. He'd made the mistake of joking about it with an old friend of his, who just so happened to be a previous chatty client I'd dealt with nearly three months ago. The old cunt hadn't shut his mouth about it, so it was easy to start digging up information once I'd started.

Harold has been married three times, has seven daughters and two sons between all those wives, and he'd pimped the majority of them out to his rich asshole friends from the moment they all reached the ripe age of thirteen. To make matters worse, one of the wives even knows about it and takes a cut from the profit.

One of the daughters committed suicide at the age of seventeen, another one of them has a bunch of mental health issues including anorexia, and one of the sons despises all forms of affection and is basically a robot. The sad thing about the son is he would probably end up on my list one day, because his anger issues towards women are pretty fucking strong.

His mother is the one who knows what's going on, and he hates her for it.

Not that I blame him.

I make my way towards the limousine that's parked down a side alley, and I open the back door myself, not noticing any driver around. The moment I slip inside, my senses go on alert as I find Harold and who

I assume is the driver, sitting there waiting for me.

Harold smiles at me like a creep, his eyes raking over my figure.

"You are a beauty. I hope you don't mind that my friend watches."

Fuck. Looks like I'm just fucking and not killing today.

I paste on a charming smile, letting out an annoying giggle.

"Oh, that's perfectly fine! Anything extra will cost though."

The driver fumbles in his pocket and pulls out a wad of bills, practically throwing them at me.

"Can I touch you? Is that enough?"

Quite sure he's a fucking virgin, because no man throws that much money at a woman just to touch them while looking that fucking nervous. I flutter my lashes at him, biting my lip and parting my legs to tease him.

"You can have a ride too, if you want? If Mr. Aster doesn't mind, that is," I answer in a breathy voice, and Harold's smile becomes dark.

"Of course I don't mind. How about you get out of that dress and show us what we're working with," he asks, and I oblige like the good little paid whore that I am. I slip from the dress but leave the silver strappy heels on, sliding my foot up Harold's leg.

"Well? Do you like what you see, Mr. Aster?"

The driver looks ready to fucking combust at the sight of my tits, let alone my pussy being on display. Who needs underwear, right?

Harold hauls me onto his lap, smelling my neck like a weirdo.

"You smell divine. Put a condom on me," he orders, shuffling his pants down awkwardly without moving me from his lap. I accept the condom and lean back, placing it over the head and slowly rolling it down his shaft while biting my lip.

He's already groaning, so I know it won't take him long once I actually start fucking him. But things don't always go as planned.

The driver suddenly grabs both my arms and holds them tightly behind my back, chuckling in my ear.

"You don't think I know who you fucking are? You killed my dad, you little slut. Found his car burned to a crisp outside of town, his body in the back and your reaper mark left in the fucking dirt," he murmurs, and for the first time in a while, I am a little thrown at that surprise. That asshole didn't have kids, and I have no idea how that connects to Harold.

Harold grins, pinching my nipples hard.

"The thing about rich pricks like myself, is that we know other rich pricks. You're the talk of the town, Reaper. It's time that you paid for your sins," he growls, shoving a finger inside me roughly.

If he really thinks he can rape me as punishment, he has another thing coming to him. I am a pro at detaching myself from my body when it comes to sex and I just have to wait it out.

His driver keeps my arms pinned as Harold does a shitty job at punishing me with his fingers, but I'm suddenly pulled backwards and slammed down onto the seat, my face pushing into the luxury fabric and my legs are held down to stop any of my fancy ninja moves. The driver is surprisingly good at the hold he has on my arms still, but he'll lose focus and give me a window to escape soon. They always do.

Nails dig into my legs as weight lands on my back, and I take my chance to yank an arm free and swing my elbow back. There's a grunt before a fist hits me in the eye, pinning my head painfully to the seat.

"You little fucking whore! Just for that, I'm going to fuck your ass hard without lube. No teeth in my seats or I'll slit your fucking throat," Harold grits out as he scrambles to keep my arms restrained. I know this isn't going to be pleasant, so I try and relax my body to avoid too much damage happening, but the door's yanked open and I hear a gurgling sound, one I know well as a throat being slit.

"I have money! I'll give you what you want, but don't hurt me!" Harold cries, letting go of me as he pleads for his life. I realize I should be panicking too, but I peer over my shoulder and a calm washes through me.

Santos looks savage as he climbs into the car and shuts us inside, grabbing Harold by the neck and slamming him down onto the seat beside me as I sit up a fraction.

"I don't give a fuck about your filthy money. No one touches my fucking baby girl!" He seethes, not hesitating before digging his blade into Harold's throat, hacking it open so that blood spills all over the place. Between the driver and Harold, there's blood everywhere, and it's not until their bodies stop moving that Santos' eyes flick to me, a mix of emotions in there that twist my stomach slightly.

"You're mine," he states clearly, his hand twitching as he grips the knife firmly still. I reach for him, uncurling his fingers from the weapon and tugging him towards me, but it's a tight fit with the two dead assholes slumped on the seat with us.

"Yeah, Santos. I'm your girl," I whisper, a pained groan coming from him before his lips crash against mine and he fucking consumes me. His hands roam my skin, and a grunt leaves him as I reach for his belt and free his dick from his pants.

I shuffle back, making room for him between my legs, and his eyes darken at the sight of my back pressed against the dead dudes, their blood still drying on my skin.

He wastes no time as he hooks his arms under the back of my knees and lifts them, slamming into me forcefully and without mercy. I scream, the delicious pain licking at my fucking soul as he rearranges my insides.

I throw my head back as he slides a hand between us to rub my clit.

I fall apart from under him, with god and the dead dudes as my witnesses, and I can't help myself as I grab Santos' throat in my hand and drag him down to kiss me. It's rough, its dirty, and I fucking love it.

His thrusts become short and sharp until he pulls out and cums on my tits, a devilish smirk on his face as he swirls his thumb through the wetness on my chest before pushing it against my lips.

I suck his thumb into my mouth, staring into his eyes as I move my tongue across his skin, and for a second I'm content. Santos is my kind of crazy, and I want to let him loose on my goddamn soul. His darkness fills me so easily, but it brings me to fucking life, too.

"Fuck, it should be illegal to be that hot," he murmurs, pulling his thumb free and drawing a wet path down my stomach until he reaches my clit again, circling it a few times before pushing two fingers inside me.

I arch up, chasing his touch as I feel more blood drip down my shoulder to mix with the cum on my chest.

His eyes remain on me as he brings me closer to release again, but just before my climax can push me over the edge, his voice hits my ears.

"Don't fucking come yet."

"I can't…"

"Fucking hold it!" He snaps, fucking my pussy with his fingers harder until I'm not even breathing anymore, trying to hold my release back. His voice is low, but his eyes are alight with desire.

"Come for me," he murmurs.

Don't have to fucking tell me twice.

I come hard, my pussy gripping his fingers as it constricts in waves, wetness gushing as he keeps finger fucking me through my screams. English words aren't even a capability at this point, it's just jumbled crap.

"Good girl," he praises, slowing his hand and leaning forward to bite my lip sharply, drawing blood. He sucks it into his mouth, running his tongue over the small cut with a groan.

"Where have you been all my fucking life? You're made for me," he whispers more to himself than me, moving back and grabbing the back of his shirt to pull it over his head. He wipes the wetness from between my legs, before cleaning my chest like it's his favourite thing to do. He might be a crazy son of a bitch, but deep down he gives a shit, and I love that I bring that out of him.

"So, now what? We can't leave this mess here," I chuckle as I observe the bloodied mess behind me. He smirks, waggling his eyebrows.

"Easy. I'll drive it out of here and we will deal with it. I'll call Darius to help."

His take charge attitude only makes me horny again, so I lick my lips and give him a coy smile.

"How about we do that again, only this time, you spank me while you choke me?"

He manhandles me until I'm straddling him, grabbing my throat hard to speak against my lips.

"Only if you ride me like a fucking porn star first, baby girl."

Best fucking plan, ever.

"God fucking damn! You guys really made a mess!" Darius hoots with laughter, but my eyes widen as I notice Santos and Selene wandering into the room behind Darius, their bodies covered in blood. Selene has Darius' shirt on, and Santos is only in his pants.

"The fuck happened?" I demand, but Santos winks at me, hooking his arm around Selene's neck to tug her against him.

"Nothing we couldn't handle."

"That's not what I fucking asked," I growl, but Darius grins, waving his hands around with enthusiasm.

"These crazy fuckers killed two people and fucked on their dead bodies! I'm a little bit upset that no one thought to call me to join in, but I'll let that shit slide since Selene's going to blow me because I said please," he exclaims, my eyes narrowing on the dress in Selene's hand.

"Is that your dress? I told you to fucking keep it safe."

She quirks an eyebrow at me like a brat, holding it out to me.

"I kept it safe. Might need a wash though. Fuck knows what's on it now," she replies, heading straight for the fridge to grab a beer. Blaze won't take his eyes off her the moment he joins us, and the scowl only deepens when Selene sits on Darius' lap and opens her legs, staring back at Blaze as Darius' hand wanders down to her swollen cunt. Santos must have really given it to her.

Jealousy surges through me, but I torture myself longer as I watch Darius touch her, his teeth dragging along her neck as she closes her eyes.

Just as he dips a finger inside her, Blaze slams a fist down on the table.

"For fuck's sake, she's not crack. How hard is it to leave her the fuck alone?!" He snarls, but Darius' lip kicks up into a taunting smirk, pushing his finger into her sinful pussy further.

"C'mon, I'll hold her legs apart while you work out some of that anger, if you want? You really gotta get laid, bro. You're starting to get wrinkles from all that scowling you do."

I bite back a chuckle, moving over to them and hauling Selene to her feet.

"Go and shower, then meet back down here so we can talk, alright?"

"We can talk first," she argues, but I run my fingers through her hair and tug her head back to stare up at me.

"We can't, because I'm going to fuck you if you don't go and wash up and put some pants on. Take Santos, he needs a shower too," I offer, stopping the argument easily.

She grins, crooking her finger at Santos.

"Come on, baby cakes. You and I are going for playtime in the shower."

I asked for that, honestly.

Why the fuck didn't I offer to help wash her?

Santos tosses her over his shoulder and carries her up the hallway with a sharp spank on her ass, and Darius follows them with his eyes. He turns to me when they're out of sight, pouting again. He was just as whipped as that other crazy fucker.

"Can I go too? Please?"

"Since you asked so nicely, I guess…," I manage to get out before he tears up the hallway as if I'll change my mind.

"You know we won't see them for hours now, right?" Blaze snarks, sitting in the chair and snatching the beer Selene left behind, downing it with annoyance. Darius wasn't kidding, Blaze needs to get laid pronto before he self-combusts with rage.

I shrug, pretending I don't give a shit but in reality I am craving to join them.

Darius and Santos are on a different kink level than I am, but there is something about Selene that makes me forget all about that shit, because if she has pleasure written all over her face from things they're doing to her, I'd nearly be down for anything.

Blaze is wrong.

Selene is like fucking crack, and she has the power to turn me into a junkie for life.

Chapter Twenty-Three

Selene

J watch as Darius starts the shower, his back muscles flexing as he adjusts the temperature, and his shirt rides up to show the beginnings of a large tribal tattoo. I bite my lip to hold in a moan and hear Santos chuckle beside me.

"You're looking at him like a piece of meat."

"He has one chunk of meat I'm most interested in." I shrug. "But my fucking pussy is dicked out right now and I'm not sure what the fuck you guys want from me."

"Your ass is good though, no?" Darius asks as he looks over his shoulder.

"And that pretty little mouth," Santos chimes in.

Fuck. I may be exhausted but the thought of being alone right now is a bit depressing. I'm tired of being alone. Since my sister disappeared and I killed my mother, I've only ever been alone.

"Let's see if you can earn it," I wink at them and strip off the shirt.

My skin is itchy from the dried blood and cum, but defiling those bodies was the best thing I've done in a while. It's time to celebrate.

I step into the warm spray of water and watch as Santos hops out of his pants to quickly join me. Darius leans back against the counter and crosses his arms over his chest.

"Are you coming in?" I ask as I dip my hair back under the spray.

"I'm a big man, Selene." His voice takes on a mischievous tone. "And you two are bloodied. When you're nice and clean, I'm fucking that tight asshole."

Well then, I better get a fucking move on.

I quickly clean my hair and body, all the while Santos has his hands on my tits or his fingers in my pussy. Then I move aside for his turn. I get out and Darius wraps me up in a plush towel, then kisses me softly.

"That's the sweetest thing you're getting," he warns before his lips curl up against mine. "After this, it's all debauchery."

"I'm done!" Santos turns off the water and jumps out of the shower.

His wet body plows into mine from behind and I'm sandwiched between them. All hard, bulging muscles touching my soft curves.

Darius' big hands land on my shoulders and he gently pushes me down to my knees.

"I'll take what you promised me now," he grins.

I go to my knees and Santos rips the towel off me.

"I'll hold her head steady," he chuckles as his fingers grip my strands.

Darius has his pants down and cock out in a flash, it's hard and angry looking.

"Open wide," he says as he presses the wide mushroom head to my mouth.

I do as I'm told and moan as soon as his taste invades my mouth. His salty flavor rushes over my tongue and I slurp around the head of his cock. My tongue pays extra attention to the rough ridge under the head and I feel his legs relax as a rough groan leaves his mouth.

"Feels good, huh?" Santos asks him as his fingertips massage my scalp.

"Fuck yes." Darius replies.

"Are we done with the sweet shit?" Santos growls. "Can I fuck you with her face now?"

Darius grunts and I clench my eyes shut, knowing exactly what's coming. Santos digs into my scalp and forcefully begins thrusting my face onto Darius' dick.

"Holy fuck," Darius groans. "You sure do know how to suck dick, Santos."

"You already knew that."

Huh? What?

My confusion leaves me unprepared for when Santos shoves my face right into Darius' pelvis, his cock slamming down my throat. I gag and my hands push against Darius' thighs, trying to create some space.

Santos pulls my head back and I have about two seconds to inhale before I'm shoved right back against Darius again. I'm fucking furious at being manhandled like this and my anger takes on a new level when Santos pulls me back.

I forcefully throw my head back and slam it into Santos' dick. He drops behind me like a sack of potatoes, cursing me colorfully. Then I jab my fist into Darius' lower belly and glare when he pitches forward on a harsh exhale.

"You motherfuckers," I seethe as I get to my feet. "I'm down for rough play, I fucking like it, but do not - and I mean do not - force it on me."

I get to my feet, shoving Darius back, and kicking Santos in the chest.

"You're lucky I'm not fucking gutting you," I growl and stomp out of the bathroom into my room. "I may be a whore but I am not your fucking property to do as you please!" I yell at them.

I throw on yet another pair of Zander's boxers and a t-shirt and make my way back to the kitchen. Zander and Blaze are having what looks to be an intense conversation and I stop in the doorway.

Blaze sees me first and rolls his eyes, the scar tugging his features a bit to the side. "Over so soon?"

"Your men may or may not be suffering in the washroom." I shrug and walk in further. "Had to teach them a fucking lesson in consent."

"Whores require consent?" Blaze narrows his eyes.

"Blaze…" Zander grits out in warning.

"Especially whores," I shrug and plop my ass on the chair beside him. "Money is our contract. Your boys were getting it for free and took advantage."

"Selene!" I hear Darius call from the hallway.

"Fuck," Zander presses his fingers to his forehead, "Here we go."

Darius storms into the kitchen naked, his face red, and his cock still hard and angry.

"Yes?" I raise my brow at him.

"We've done worse!" He exclaims, "What the fuck was all that?"

"With my permission." I hold my finger up.

Santos comes around the corner and props up against the wall, still gripping his junk. "The fuck was that?"

"What did you do?" Zander looks at them with boredom.

"They bruised my esophagus with Darius' dick and forced me to choke against his pubes," I give them a pointed look.

Santos begins to look sheepish but Darius' face only boils hotter.

"That's all part of a good cock sucking," he retorts.

"Oh yeah?" I lean my face on my hand, elbow resting on the table. "Show me what you mean."

"What?" Zander and Darius ask at the same time.

"I don't know what you mean by saying a bruised esophagus and pube choking are all part of a good cock sucking." I point from him to Santos, "So show me."

"Oh for fuck's sake," Blaze mutters and stands. "You are all so fucked up." Then he's storming out of the kitchen.

I'm gonna wear him down eventually.

Santos begins to yank down his sweatpants and Darius rolls his eyes. "You really want me to suck his dick?"

"Yeah," I nod, "and choke on it."

Darius shrugs like this is no big deal and drops to his knees, throwing me a wink over his shoulder. "Take notes."

I press my lips together to stop myself from laughing and watch as Darius grips Santos' cock in his big hand, giving it a few lazy pumps.

My pussy clenches and I turn to see Zander's eyes on me. I look away from him and back to Darius just as he begins to fucking swallow Santos' cock. I mean fucking swallow all the way down his throat, his nose nestled deep in pubes, and his hand massaging the balls.

This isn't his first rodeo and the thought has me standing slowly. I may be fucking sore but my pussy is dripping as I watch them. Santos has his head tossed back against the wall and his hands in Darius' hair as he moans loudly.

Then Darius does indeed begin to choke on Santos' dick, gagging loudly. The moan escapes my mouth before I can stop it and Zander's hands encircle my waist dragging me towards where he's sitting.

"You like that, baby?" He whispers and I nod, my eyes still glued to Darius.

Zander pulls his boxers down my legs and adjusts me to straddle his waist. His finger slides through my pussy and he groans at how wet I am.

"Guys," he looks to Darius and Santos. "Don't fucking stop, she's loving this."

They don't bother to answer him, too lost in their own moment, and I begin to grind down onto Zander's fingers.

"You want me inside you, baby?" He whispers in my ear. "Fucking you while Darius sucks Santos' cock?"

"Yes," I moan and watch as Zander pulls his cock from his pants.

He lifts me by the waist and slowly impales me along his wide cock. I begin to grind on Zander while Darius' sucking noises fills the room.

"Fuck!" I exclaim as my pussy squeezes Zander's length.

I begin to ride him faster, my pussy's sucking sounds fucking rivaling Darius'.

"Oh fuck no," I hear Darius growl just before I'm lifted off of Zander's lap. "We worked hard for this, there's no way you're giving it to this asshole."

Zander leisurely continues to pump his glistening cock and grins.

"All of us," I pant in Darius' arms. "Bedroom now."

Darius heads there, his long strides eating up the space in no time, and I hear the others following close behind. I have never had three guys at once, I haven't even had double penetration, but I'm more turned on by the idea than I am apprehensive.

Darius falls back on the bed, keeping me straddled on top, and motions towards the side table.

"Get the lube and condoms."

"No need for lube." Santos murmurs.

I hear the slide of the drawer and the crinkle of condom wrappers, but I can't look because Darius has his tongue down my throat. I can taste the musky flavor of Santos in his mouth and moan while my hips search out his cock.

I feel him slide a condom on and he wastes no time sliding deep inside me.

"Fuck," I pull away from his mouth.

I feel a sharp sting on my ass cheek and whip my head around in time to see Zander rubbing his hand against a brand new cut courtesy of Santos and wiping it down the length of his cock. That's a fucking first, blood as lube. Then Santos has his hand wiping my blood from the cut to my asshole.

I clasp my ass cheeks together at the sticky feeling.

"No, no baby girl." Zander says from behind me. "This one is mine."

The bed dips to our left and I turn away from Zander in time to see Santos' cock bob in my face. I open my mouth and he pushes inside, this time giving me time to adjust to his size. At the same time, I feel Zander's wide cock slowly begin to stretch open my puckered hole, the burn immediate, but the slippery texture of the blood making the intrusion easier.

As soon as his head breaches the tight muscle, he pushes himself in, and I'm moaning around Santos' cock.

"Fuck," Santos groans. "Make her do that again."

Darius pulls out, then slams back in, Zander pulls out, then slams back in, and their rhythm makes me a whimpering mess around Santos' cock.

"Fuck," his fingers curl into my hair. "I'm going to cum down that pretty throat."

No sooner than his words leave his mouth, he does just that, the salty, musky taste of him invading my mouth. I swallow him down and suck him softly as he pulls out from between my soft lips. He falls over onto his back on the bed and watches as Darius wraps his hand around my neck, pulling me in for a deep kiss.

It's like he's licking Santos' taste right out of my mouth, and the thought of him swallowing Santos' dick has me almost blacking out as my orgasm bowls me over.

"So... tight..." Darius grunts up into me and groans his release.

He keeps himself lodged inside of me as Zander continues to punish my asshole.

"She's so tight," he agrees and his thrusts become sloppy and erratic. "So tight."

Then he thrusts in once more, spilling himself deep in me, and his fingers leaving bruises on my hips.

I fall forward on top of Darius and immediately pass out.

Chapter Twenty-Four

Zander

I have Darius and Santos with me for the drop, the three of us having been summoned by my piece of shit father. He's never liked Blaze and I always get a thrill of satisfaction when he cringes at his scar.

Blaze is home babysitting our newest obsession. Selene is highly unpredictable and I can't have her seducing her way into things, so that leaves Blaze who is unaffected by her charms to keep her occupied.

Tonight the shipment is coming by Mack himself and this only ever happens when he has something special aboard. Special as in kids. That's right, kids, young too, like ages ranging from five to sixteen. Those shipments are my father's favourite since he gets a large price tag for them.

"I fucking hate doing this." Darius kicks at a stone at his feet.

"I need to see how many are on this shipment," I explain. "We have to figure out how to get them out of here in three days."

My father has an export container docking in three days to send his shipment overseas into Morocco.

"Yeah," Darius scrubs his hand down his face. "I know."

Santos wets up the spliff in his hand and sparks the end, the cloying scent of marijuana attacking our sense of smell. It's a must for us to get a little stoned for these drop offs. It helps us pack away the emotions and just gather the information needed to help the helpless.

We pass the spliff between us until there's nothing left and Santos crushes it under his boot. The sun has long since gone down and the moon illuminates the trees and bushes lining this estate's driveway. When my mother was killed, or like my father likes to say, had a terrible accident, I barely stayed in this house. Her angry spirit haunts the place and my fucking nightmares.

"He's here," Santos says quietly.

We all turn our heads and watch as an eighteen wheeler pulls into the driveway carrying a large cargo container behind it. It slowly moves up the driveway as Santos and Darius move to my flanks. I need to get this shit done and get the fuck back home to a pussy I am now addicted to. Oh, and an asshole too apparently.

We watch as Mack parks and hops down from the driver's seat. He's a fat cunt and I cringe as I watch his knees take the fucking impact of his obesity.

"Boys!" His rough voice calls out, the fucker smokes two packs of cigarettes a day and he fucking sounds like it. "I have the goods tonight!"

His hands rub together and I fist mine at my sides. I want to smash my knuckles into his fat, ruddy face and watch as he spits out teeth from the force.

"Let's get it done," Darius calls out. "I got a juicy cunt waiting for me at home."

"Hold your horses." Mack comes to stand in front of us and it's at that moment I hear a low cry of a child inside the container.

My teeth crack from grinding them so fucking hard.

"Hear that?" Mack grins, his front teeth brown and his bottom teeth missing. "Those children are pristine, I haven't even had my way with any of them."

"Let's get it done," Santos growls, repeating Darius' sentiment all while flipping his knife in his hand.

Mack, like the stupid fucking idiot he is, doesn't heed his warning and throws his head back with a cackle.

"I remember being young like you boys. Life was grand, me and my boys would run the town, and fuck every girl." His fat pink tongue dabs at his bottom lip. "Oh man, those were the days."

I bet he raped all the girls because I can't imagine anyone wanting this piece of shit. I pull out the pieces of rolled up papers from my inside jacket pocket and read over the details.

"Twenty-four women, six young men, five young boys, and seven young girls, correct?" I ask him.

"Nice haul, huh?" He chuckles.

"What a thing to be proud of." I make sure the sarcasm is heavy in my voice.

"Listen kid," he reaches into his jacket pocket and pulls out a pack of smokes. "This will be your company when your father is done, you better start to enjoy, and enjoy the money that comes with it."

I watch as his short stubby fingers places a cigarette between those swollen bluish-red lips and lights the tip. His first inhale takes in a quarter of the smoke and he exhales directly into my face. My first instinct is to reach forward, but luckily Darius throws his arm across my chest.

"Easy, Bro," his voice is low. "Now's not the time."

He's right, we need to get this done because the hit my father has out on us could be anywhere and us being out in the open for too long could cost us our fucking lives. My father wouldn't have the Diablos anywhere near his shipment but that doesn't mean they aren't waiting for when we're finished here.

I nod at Santos and he opens the passenger side door of the car and pulls out a briefcase. The fucker is filled with enough money to feed a small country and it's painful to watch it being handed over to this dirty cunt.

"Thanks boys." His toothless grin has me choking back a gag. "Let's begin the offloading."

He opens the back and we peer inside at the bodies huddled together, all with burlap bags over their heads, and not much clothing on. Some are barefoot and even though I smoked that joint, I still want to rip Mack's fucking head off.

I watch as Darius begins to line them up and Santos guides each of them inside the house, then down to the basement like all the other times we've been through this. I stand out here with the biggest piece of shit and keep an eye on our surroundings.

The fucker lights what must be the tenth smoke in ten minutes and begins another fucking story about how he was in college. I don't fucking give a shit and I can't wait until I am able to slide my knife through his throat.

"Then your father thought it would be a good idea to become partners and we then became millionaires by the age of twenty-three..." Blah blah blah.

I give the front of the house a quick perimeter scan and nearly jump out of my skin when I watch a familiar form, completely decked out in black, and a hood up over her head rush around the side of the house.

What the fuck is Selene doing here? And where the fuck is Blaze?

Every man is fucking predictable, even the ones that swear up and down that they don't want you, and I just proved that point tonight. Blaze is indeed blazing hot under that deep umber skin and prominent pinkish-white scar, and he is on the verge of giving in to me.

I know exactly what the guys are up to tonight because I have filthy Mack's itinerary for the next few months and I know tonight is the biggest shipment of underage children this year. Even if I wanted to, I can't miss this opportunity, and I needed to get out from under Blaze's thumb. So, I had two options, kill the fucker, or get him riled up and leave the room.

Option one would've gotten me in hot water with the others, so I went with option two, and as per usual Blaze stormed from the room. I hadn't even gotten to sinking my fingers in my exposed pussy yet, just a few swipes through my folds.

I Ubered to a few blocks from the Walton mansion and walked the rest of the way on foot. That's when I stumbled upon a car with two shady looking fuckers sitting outside the gates. They looked way too similar to the guys that rushed Santos' house the night of the party and I couldn't take the chance that they would try something on my boys.

Yeah, I fucking said it, my boys.

I approached the open passenger side window and leaned in seductively. Before the guy could say a fucking thing, I had my gun to his head and his brains exploding on both me and the driver.

After that, it was easy to get the second guy talking since his face was coated in his buddy's blood. They were the Diablos and on a stake out mission to collect info for some Antonio dude. Once I had that, I blew his forehead open wide and for the fun of it, drew my scythe into the brain matter clotting along the dash.

Hopefully, that sends a clear enough message to this Antonio.

Now, as I make my way up the driveway, I spot Zander standing with the disgusting sloth Mack. He looks like he's fucking vibrating with anger and I can feel the tension even from over fifty feet away. Mack looks completely engrossed with his own conversation and neither notices as I pass behind the rows of trees, approaching the side of the house.

I made sure to be completely covered in black so that I would blend better and not catch the eyes of onlookers. Another good thing about coming here tonight? Henry Walton turns off all surveillance during a drop off, so there is absolutely zero evidence if he's ever investigated.

Lucky me, not so lucky, Mr. Walton.

I see Santos and Darius ushering the women and children inside, so I slip by them and down the side of the house. I see the door obscured by climbing vines and slam my fist through the small window. I know this narrow doorway is an old servants entrance and that this side of the house is rarely used.

I slip inside and look around the empty mudroom, the dark shadows concealing me well. I know exactly where Henry is and getting there will be no problem but getting by those other three pains in my ass, will be the hard part.

This mudroom leads to a smaller kitchen that's long been abandoned. It looks like it was used for the servants to cook and eat in, pretentious assholes. I step out of the kitchen and I'm immediately inside a small living room. There's a door straight ahead leading to a corridor and back into the front of the mansion and a door to my right that leads to an old wine cellar.

I turn to the right and unlock the bolt, cringing when it scrapes loudly, and open the door. I hear the shuffle of feet and a few murmured voices telling me that they are indeed keeping the fresh meat in the cellar. I know beyond the cellar is a small office and then a stairwell leading up to the main kitchen in the house.

In that small office I will find Henry, taking accounts of what he's receiving. I can hear both Darius and Santos below, mumbling about something, and leading the line into the cellar. If they even catch the smallest glimpse of me, I know they'll recognize me, and to be fucking honest I would be pissed if they didn't.

Knowing they're there, I sit at the top of the stairs and wait it out. I hear a few muffled sobs and some not so muffled children's cries, breaking my fucking heart. Soon, I tell myself. Soon, I will have them all safe, they just have to endure this next step, and if they've survived this long, I know they're strong enough to keep going.

I'm sitting on that cold concrete stair for at least a half an hour when I hear Zander call out from the other stairway.

"Darius, Santos. Let's go, we got shit to discuss."

"Make sure you're back here when the export is ready!" Henry calls out to him.

Export.

Like they are fucking cattle.

I can't wait until I get that motherfucker alone and show him just what I think about his import/export business. I hear the door upstairs close and I continue to sit on the fucking stairs for another fifteen minutes.

Chapter Twenty-Five

Zander

"I saw Selene go into the house," I tell Darius and Santos as we stand outside on the driveway.

"That's fucking impossible," Santos huffs.

"Blaze wouldn't take his fucking eyes off her."

"Unless she killed him," Darius offers and gets an excited look in his eye. It's the same one he gets whenever he thinks about our girl.

"Call him," Santos says as he begins to light another spliff.

"No need," I hear Blaze's distinct growl from behind us.

I turn and cross my arms over my chest. "Bro, why did you let her come here?"

"Let her?" There's a wild look in his eye. Something I haven't seen in a long time. "The bitch got the jump on me."

"She's inside," I nod towards the house. "How the fuck are we getting her out?"

"We?" Blaze's lip curls up in anger, his scar pulling at his left eye. "I'm dealing with her tonight. You three go on back to the house."

I sigh, knowing nothing is going to stand in his way now that he's set his mind to it.

I give him a nod, motioning for the other two to follow me as Blaze scowls and stalks into the house, and I hope to God he doesn't fucking kill her. She pushes all of his buttons, so I'm not surprised he's starting to snap.

We climb into the car and I start the engine, glancing over at Darius.

"You think he's going to kill her?"

Santos hoots in the back, slapping his knee for dramatics.

"As if. Our girl would win that fight easy with her fucking eyes shut. I kind of want to stick around and watch it happen. She's always horny after a kill, and my dick gets rock hard seeing her covered in their blood."

"You're disgusting," I mutter, mentally cursing my dick as it jumps behind my zipper at the image that's now in my head.

We drive down the driveway and I do a second take when I notice a car parked by the gates. The guys spot it too, and just as Santos pulls his gun out, preparing to rain bullets between the two cars, I spot the blood splatter all over the windshield.

"What the fuck?" Darius murmurs from the back, waiting for me to pull over before carefully climbing from the car to inspect the situation.

Santos lets out a low whistle as he walks around the car, peeking in the window to see the mayhem inside.

"Diablos?" Darius questions, raising an eyebrow as Santos opens the door to get a closer look. They are practically unrecognizable, but I recognize one from the night they went through the fucking house and attacked us.

"Who the fuck…" I mumble before my eyes zero in on the dash to see the scythe drawn into the bloodied brain matter. "Selene did this."

Santos groans, rubbing his dick through his pants, but Darius frowns.

"You sure?"

"Yep. She left her reaper mark," I nod, motioning to the symbol.

"Well fuck, we agreed to keep her yeah? Because I'm not letting her go. Starting to think she's crazier than I am. I'm impressed," Santos grins, slamming the door and moving around to me. Selene and Santos are dangerous together, but the fuckers are perfect for each other.

I roll my eyes and jerk my chin towards our car.

"C'mon, let's get out of here and wait for our girl and the angry asshole to get home."

I can't wait for her to get her psycho ass home so I can get her under me again.

The basement becomes still and I can hear a few sniffles here and there, but for the most part everything has died down. I can hear papers shuffling every now and then, telling me Henry is still in his office and that suits me just fucking fine.

I head down the stairs and cut a quick left at the bottom, entering a room designed for pleasure or torture, depending on the person's perspective. This is Henry's pleasure room and it's his sex slaves' torture room.

I look around and fucking almost lose it when I see swings and chains all over, blood still along their surfaces. Then I hear a whimper and see about twenty people and children crammed into a cage that's no more than eight feet across and ten in length.

I hold my finger to my mouth, praying they listen, and slowly creep towards them. A woman comes forward, a child clutched to her thigh, and reaches her hand out.

"We just want to go home," she whispers.

"I know," I nod. "I'm here to help, I just need you to be very quiet. Okay?"

She nods.

"Can you pass it along to everyone? To please stay calm and quiet?" I ask her and she nods once again then disappears through the throng.

I back away and look along the adjacent wall seeing a ton of floggers, whips, and just about every sexual torture device you can think of. Even big ass strap on dongs.

The guy is a fucking parasite and I can't wait to give him a taste of what he's been dishing out for decades.

I walk back to the cage and the woman stands there wide eyed and shaking. "Everyone is going to be quiet," she whispers.

"Perfect," I nod and notice a huge padlock on the door. I look around and find a huge set of keys sitting on the table, this fucking guy is just so sure of himself.

I grab the keys and unlock the gate. "I need you all to go back up the way you came. Wait for me on the far left of the front gates. Stay together and I will be out when I'm done. Understood?"

She nods and murmurs the instructions to the rest.

"Be very quiet," I remind them as they begin to shuffle out in a single file.

I watch as they head up the stairs, back out the way they came, and then I go back inside the torture room, lifting myself up to the table, waiting for Henry.

He doesn't keep me waiting long at all, I bet the fucker wanted to come in here and begin his torture, and I thank the fucking stars everyone was quick and efficient.

He strides in and stops suddenly when he sees me lounging on the table.

"Selene?" His brows crash together and his eyes shift quickly to the cage.

When he sees it empty, his eyes snap back to mine. "What the fuck did you do?"

"No Henry," I tsk as I hop off the table. "What the fuck have you done?"

His face turns beet red and he bares his teeth as he storms towards me. I whip my gun out of my pocket and point it right between his fucking eyes.

"Now, now," I grin at him, "take it easy. Let's have a little chat."

"Where is my fucking shipment?" He snarls as he stares down the barrel of my gun.

"Where is my fucking sister?" I exclaim and his eyes widen at my very first show of emotion. "Don't push me Henry, I want you to die, and it would be so fucking easy to squeeze this trigger and watch your head explode."

His hands slowly begin to rise, like the dumb fucker just figured out I'm fucking serious, and I roll my eyes.

"What sister, Selene?" His voice becomes eerily calm, like he's trying to soothe me.

"Her name was Jan," I narrow my gaze on him. "Sold by a meth addict woman for a thousand dollars."

"Look, I have my ledger out on my desk," he points behind him towards the office. "I'll help you, but I need you to bring everyone back."

"Wrong answer!" I sing-song and aim the gun to his knee, pulling the trigger.

Even with the silencer on, the popping noise seems to reverberate around the room, like an echo. Then Henry's screams of pain join in and I begin to sway with the melody.

"You crazy fucking bitch!" He screams as he holds the wound on his knee, blood oozing out between his fingers.

"Now you're beginning to get the right answers!" I giggle maniacally and prance on the spot. "Shall I reward you, Henry?"

He's moaning with pain, and when his eyes finally meet mine, I see the look of resignation in them. Like the fucker knows I'm here to kill him and that this was my plan all along.

"Get up on the table, Henry." My voice sounds as sweet as fucking sugar.

He shakes his head and let's it drop to his chest, "No."

"Oh no!" I exclaim, "That was another wrong answer!"

I cock the gun and his head snaps up quickly, "No! Wait!" But I've already put pressure on the trigger and there's no turning back.

The bullet slams into his shoulder and he falls back onto the concrete floor. He begins to writhe on the ground and I begin to twist a lock of hair around my finger while I wait for him to fucking stop screaming.

"Henry," I chastise. "I need you up on the table, please." Sweet as fucking pie.

He slowly rises to his feet, his hand clutching the wound on his shoulder and putting no weight on his shot knee.

"I need a doctor," he pants as he hops to the table and I come up behind him to shove him forward.

He hits the table with a grunt, and shouts when his knee feels the impact. Must hurt like a fucking bitch.

I hold the gun to his head and he stills when he feels the cold metal.

"Stay on your stomach and remove your pants," I speak low and slowly.

"What?" He mumbles and I press the gun harder into his skull. "Okay!"

He does as I say and struggles to remove his pants, his moans of pain making me laugh.

"Underwear too, Henry." I slap his ass. "Be a good little whore."

I see his shoulders begin to shake and I choke back a laugh at the thought of him crying. I can just imagine how many women and children he had in this very same predicament, crying just the same, and on this table no less. The thought is validating and I feel almost vindicated.

Almost.

He pulls off his underwear and I hear a quiet sob escape his chest. They all cry at the end, once they realize they can't beg their way out of it, they cry for mercy. I have yet to show any one of my targets mercy.

I round the top of the table and drag my gun across his head with me. Once I reach the other side, I see his eyes are tightly shut and he has tears coursing down his cheeks.

Boo hoo, little bitch.

"Henry," I say sweetly. "What's your favorite piece here on the board?"

His eyes open wide and he looks up at me, "No, don't."

"No? Don't?" I mock him. "Why would you purchase these if you don't like them yourself?"

His sobs become harder and I cackle as I watch him.

"I like this." I reach my hand out and brush my fingers along the large black silicone strap on.

He just shakes his head as I pull it off the board.

"No," he grits out and begins to lift himself off the table.

"Not a good idea, Henry," I tsk as I slam the handle of the gun into his temple, effectively knocking him out.

I walk down to the foot of the table and drag his body down until he's bent over in an easily accessible position. Again, the feeling of sweet revenge courses through me and I chuckle as I strap the foot long dong onto my body.

A foot long.

Twelve fucking inches of pain and this is what he loved to serve up to his victims. Well, I'm about to find out what it's like to have a swinging cock and plunge it into a tight hole. Every man's desire.

I pull apart his ass cheeks and line myself up, which is a lot harder to do when you're this well hung. The fucking thing swings all over the damn place and when you think you're about to hit bullseye, you tap a sac instead.

Finally, I hit his tiny pink puckered hole and begin to push forward. It's tough to do because it's just so small and this fucking dong has the girth of a fucking eggplant. But I'm nothing if not a go getter and I keep at it. I breach the tight circle of muscle and then it's the home stretch, see what I did there? Stretch?

I begin to laugh as I watch his asshole *stretch* and then I slam in all the fucking way. He comes back to consciousness with a scream and I pull out a bit only to slam right the fuck back in. He's trying to kick but he has one injured knee and movement is just about impossible without a lot of pain. Plus, I can imagine he's losing a lot of blood, and now adding his asshole to the list of wounds, only increases that.

I can hear the drips of blood hitting the floor and I can't tell if it's coming from his knee or his asshole. I've literally ripped him a new one.

His body slumps forward again, the pain having him lose consciousness and I figure my torture session is done for the day. It's really unfortunate that Henry couldn't take a good pegging, he sure was good at giving it himself. I pull out of him, remove the strap on, and let it hit the ground with a thud, blood sprinkles out with the impact.

Ouch.

I pull him the rest of the way off the table and watch as his body hits the concrete with a sickening crack. I stand still, watching to see if his chest still moves with his breaths, and curse when it moves slightly. This fucker is still alive.

I pull my knife out of my pocket and crouch down over his body, cutting open his shirt to expose his muscular torso. Same build as Zander.

I dig my knife into his unmarred skin and begin carving my sigil, the reaper's scythe. I want everyone to know Reaper Incarnate was here.

"What the fuck is going on?" I hear a familiar angry voice behind me.

Great, the fucker found me.

R E A P E D

THE REAPER INCARNATE

Chapter Twenty-Six

Selene

"**B**laze," I call out to him. "I'm a little busy. Can you come back in fifteen?"

I hear his heavy combat boots hit the concrete floor with each step.

Thud.

Thud.

He's taking his time making his way over to me, like maybe my erratic behavior is scaring him, and I can't help but feel a bit of excitement at that thought.

"This was your end game." His voice is gruff but the anger is dissipating.

"He killed my sister." I say quietly. "There's a ledger, probably in his office, that has all the names of the people he's ever... acquired. Her name has to be in it."

"Is he dead?" He slowly crouches beside me.

"Almost."

He looks at what I'm carving into his chest, "You really are the fucking Reaper Incarnate."

"I said I was."

He grabs a hold of my chin and forces me to look away from the bleeding scythe. "Finish him off."

"Will Zander hate me?" My voice sounds small and the most vulnerable it's been since my sister disappeared.

"No, just disappointed he didn't get to do it himself."

I look back down at Henry and watch as his eyes crack open. The breath rattles in his chest and he opens his mouth to speak but I don't give him the fucking chance as I slam my knife down into his throat.

The blood sprays up and lands on my face, hitting Blaze's too. I watch as his eyes darken and rove all over my face, taking in the blood.

"You look like a warrior." It's the nicest I've heard him speak. "You *are* a fucking warrior."

Then his mouth is on mine and I can taste the metallic flavor of Henry's blood mixed with Blaze. It sets me off and I push him to his ass and straddle his waist. The buildup between us has been rising towards this very moment and it's threatening to blow, taking down everything around us.

I want his hands on my skin and his cock in my pussy. I'm nearly soaked all the way through my pants just thinking about it.

"Don't do this with me, only to fucking pull back later," I snarl into his mouth, then lick at the scar that starts at his top lip and ends at his temple. "Because I will fucking kill you."

He pulls away and looks into my eyes, his dark skin blooming with a red undertone. "I think you know as well as I do that this is what was always going to happen."

His plush mouth is back on mine and I'm grinding down onto him, desperately wanting him inside me. I stand up abruptly and begin to pull my leggings down, noticing they are saturated in Henry's blood. My skin has a sheen of red and it makes me feel more wanton, greedy for Blaze's cock.

He's in just as much of a rush as he stands in a flurry, discarding his clothes. Then he's standing in front of me, gloriously naked, and scars riddling his entire body.

He sees me looking at them and shrugs, "We all have a story to tell."

I get to his cock and it stands proud, a piece of metal gleaming at its tip. I look down to the dong on the floor and back to his cock, comparing the size and swallowing in anticipation or fucking fear. There's not much of a difference and I want it inside me even though I'm fucking scared of it going inside me.

"Get on all fours." He demands and I look down to the puddle of blood, slowly pooling across the floor. "Go on." He nods at it.

Should be fucking disgusting right? It should make me dry up like the Sahara Desert, right? Well not this bitch, I'm practically coming as I kneel down into Henry's still warm blood, and plop forward on my hands, his blood splattering on my chest. It's still warm and it pools around my hands, while I stare into Henry's dead eyes.

I feel Blaze kneel behind me and his fingers search out my core. "Fuck, you're so wet."

I push back against him and hear his dark chuckle.

"Do you think this little pussy can take my cock?" He asks as he sinks two fingers deep inside me.

The coarse feeling of his fingers against my soft insides feels rough and so fucking amazing, I continue to ride his fingers, feeling my wetness coating my thighs. I want more.

His thumb hits my clit and I moan loudly at the contact, "Fuck Blaze. Don't stop."

He chuckles and presses his fingers in farther, rubbing furiously against my bundle of nerves. I hang my head and pant, my orgasm building.

"Look into his face when you come," Blaze demands. "Show him just how much you've conquered."

I scream and look into Henry's face as I come hard around Blaze's fingers, my pussy convulsing quickly. I barely have time to come down, when I feel his wide cock begin to push its way inside me. My pussy is slick and the greedy bitch moves to accommodate him, sucking him inside.

"Fuck," it's his turn to curse.

I snort and begin to push back against him, his cock spreading me in the most delicious way. Finally, after what feels like ages, he bottoms out inside me and I moan at the feeling of being filled past the brim.

"So wet, my little whore," he moans deeply.

Little whore. Fuck, he makes that sound so hot. He pulls out and begins to push back in, his piercing scraping along my walls. The feeling of it gliding over that certain spot inside me has me cresting quickly, and I can feel my lower belly gathering heat.

"Can I cum inside you?" He asks and I want to moan at the thought of it.

"Yes," I pant and scream out when he picks up the pace.

My core coils so tight, I curl my fingers in the thick blood, and scream Blaze's name when it snaps, a flood of sensation washing over my whole body. I'm squeezing him tightly inside me, making it hard for him to move, and he lightly grinds into me until I'm coming back down.

"Ready?" He whispers as he curls over my body, his bloody hand curling into my hair.

Ready for what?

He rears back up and I look over my shoulder, watching as he grins at me. The fucker is gorgeous. I'm busy watching his face in awe, unprepared when I'm almost slammed forward into Henry's face at Blaze's new punishing rhythm.

He's pounding into me, chasing his orgasm, and eliciting noises from my pussy I've never heard before. His fingers dig into my hips and I'm a whimpering mess as he uses me roughly. He slams in one final time, groaning as I feel him jerk inside of me, and I try desperately to catch my fucking breath.

"I'm now a crack pussy addict like the rest of those dumb fuckers," he growls as he pulls out. "I get it now. This pussy is fucking crack."

"I knew it was just a matter of time," I grin and get to my feet.

I have Henry's blood all over me and it's hard to fucking get my clothes back on.

Fuck! I suddenly remember I have people waiting outside for me.

"Fuck!" I try jumping into my pants.

"What?" Blaze asks, as he tries pulling his shirt down.

"I have people waiting for me." I grab up my trench and pull my knife out of Henry's throat.

"I had them pile into a cargo van I asked a friend to bring by. There was one girl who was adamant about staying until you got back up. I didn't want them in the fucking cold."

I fly forward and wrap my arms around him as he tentatively wraps his around my waist.

"Thank you," I mumble into his chest. "Thank you for being here."

"I would've been down here sooner if I didn't have to help them," he grumbles, back to his grumpy self.

"Then you would've walked in on me fucking Henry up the ass." I pull away and grin up at him.

As much as he tries, he can't stop the smile that widens his mouth, and I'm almost shocked as he belts out a laugh.

"Kind of wish I did see it though." He says through the laughter. "Let's grab that ledger and I'll get Santos and Darius back here to clean him up." He nods at Henry.

"Can you get upstairs to the people waiting for me?" I widen my eyes at him, trying to emulate the innocence my blue eyes give me, "make sure they're not freaking out and I'll grab the ledger?"

His calloused fingers clasp my chin and he hauls me into his body, his lips crash down on mine. I moan into his kiss, the abrasive feeling I lock away as being uniquely Blaze's, and my fingers snare into his shirt, pulling him in even closer. His plush mouth at odds with the rough way he kisses has me ready to rip his clothes off again. How did we go this long without tearing into each other?

"You want to look through that ledger, for your sister, right?" He asks, his lips brushing against mine with each word.

"Yes," my voice breaks at the very same moment my heart does. I give myself the two seconds to feel it, pressing my forehead to Blaze's, and grieving for everything I'm about to lose. Two seconds and then I'm hauling up my big girl panties and pulling back to look into his eyes.

"I get it," he growls and yanks my head back by my hair, "you need your space. I'll take care of the people upstairs and then I'll meet you at home. But Selene," his voice holds something dark and dangerous in its depths, "if you're not home and naked in my bed in one hour, I will have to hunt for you." Then his face lights up with a manic grin, the scar pulling against his mouth and eye, "I'm a good hunter."

I know my grin matches his as I reply, "are we going to run a train? All five of us?" I turn and point at Henry's wall of sin, "I want to be the caboose."

He rolls his eyes and tugs on my hair again before releasing me, "Santos and Darius wouldn't complain, save your train rides for them."

He kisses me one final time, hard and quick, and then he's climbing the stairs, easily taking three at a time with his long, beautiful legs. I knew he'd give in eventually the grumpy fucker, too bad he chose now to do it.

I rush into Henry's office and squeal when I see the open grey ledger sitting there on his desk, I imagine he was adding up his newest tally. I quickly shut the thick tome, some of the pages yellowed with time, and hold it to my chest.

Janelle, I'm going to find you.

Chapter Twenty-Seven

Blaze

My knives are spread out on the bed, my clothes shoved into a knapsack, and my Glock sitting on top. I run my finger along my lip, stopping when I feel that hard ridge of skin, and gritting my teeth to force back the memories it tries to unearth. I can't think about that now, I have less than forty minutes before I embark.

"Going somewhere?" Zander's voice hits my back.

"Someone's got to go find our girl." Just those words alone have my stomach swirling in anticipation.

"What?" I can hear the panic in his voice at the prospect of losing Selene and it takes every ounce of my will not to slam my fist into his whining mouth. "Where is she?"

"I wouldn't have to hunt her if I knew, would I?"

"You let her get away." The accusation in his voice annoying the fuck out of me.

"You better not be talking about my little bloodthirsty angel." Santos crashes into the room and I groan as Darius joins not too far behind him.

"She's gone?" Darius practically wails, his eyes wide as if I told them she's dead. Santos' eyes fill with panic and confusion, not used to giving a fuck about any bitch. I have to get her back not just for my sake, but for his too, or he'll drive us mental with his moping.

"Why the fuck would she leave us? She can't just be gone!" He exclaims, his voice lethal but full of pain. Darius nudges him, promise in his tone.

"We will drag her ass back and punish her, right? She doesn't get to come into our lives like a fucking tornado, just to walk away. Fuck that."

"Do we put out an amber alert? Fuck, I need tracking dogs and a big net," Santos says in a rush, "She can't run if I throw a big net over her and hoist her over my shoulder."

"She's not a fish," Zander deadpans.

"She's slippery like one!" Santos bites back, making Darius snigger beside him.

"Listen!" I scream over their frantic protests, "she was always going to search for her sister, we knew that. What I knew and what you three should've known is that she would do it alone. She's been alone for most of her life, why would she rely on anyone now?"

That quiets them down and they stand there in contemplation.

"What do we do now?" Zander asks, "I knew I should've taken the risk of losing my dick by adding another tracker."

"You have an amazing tracker." I grin at him and finally his mouth turns up.

"When do we leave?" Santos perks up and rubs his hands together.

"No," Zander holds out his hand and cuts him off, "Blaze will find her and bring her back."

"He'll kill her." Darius points at me.

"Not if she behaves."

"He's going to kill her, our Hell Cat would never behave." Darius' nostrils flare.

"He won't kill her," Zander says slowly, "he's had a taste of her."

Darius and Santos look at me stunned and then they simultaneously begin hooting like a pair of fucking pigeons. I roll my eyes and pack up my knives, I have twenty minutes now. The anticipation coils and I can feel my senses already beginning to open up, everything sharpening as my body prepares. It's been too long since I've hunted, the training I endured as a child has lain dormant for far too long, and now I can barely hold it back.

"I can see it in your face," Zander murmurs as he comes to stand beside me, "are you going to be able to handle this? Is there a risk you'll lose yourself?"

He has every right to ask that because he was the only one to witness me losing my grip with reality. Just once and it was a very long time ago. I can taste his fear for Selene and that pisses me off, doesn't he know she can handle herself by now? Even if I do let my hunter out to play.

"It'll be fine." I grunt and stuff my knives into my bag. "I have sixteen minutes and then the time I gave her is up. I need to eat and get on the road."

"Bring her back here so I can give her ass a good lashing," Santos grins as he flicks his knife.

"Clothing optional." Darius' smile is wide.

I give a brusque nod and push past them, sliding my bag onto my shoulder. I grab an apple off the table and a bottle of water out of the fridge, I will need to put something in my belly before I lose all thoughts on necessities. I continue on to the front door and turn the handle to open it.

"Blaze," Zander calls out, halting me in my tracks, "keep us in the loop."

Not a fucking chance.

Zander

"This is a bad idea, I can feel it." Darius moans as his ass hits the couch, "they'll kill each other."

"Let's bet on it." Santos snaps his fingers, "I'm betting Selene is back here in one piece without a scratch on her."

I want to tell them to stop acting stupid and shut the fuck up, but I can't. I can't because I have no idea what's going to go down between them. They haven't seen Blaze lose himself and can't know what Selene may be facing when he finally catches up with her. I pray I'm wrong and that Selene can somehow coax him back, she was able to win him over after all.

"Then we'll put our own scratches on her," Darius' eyes light up and I know they've effectively moved on from worried to horny.

I quietly escape from their animated conversation about tying her up and cutting her open, slipping into my room and shutting the door. I pull my phone out of my back pocket and pull up Selene's contact. I hit dial and hold the phone to my ear, my foot tapping against the carpet impatiently. After nine rings, a generic voicemail comes on, and I groan. Once the beep sounds I clear my throat.

"Hey," I sound like a fucking pussy, "thought you'd be home by now, call me."

There, maybe she'll think we're not onto her and call me back. Or maybe, I'm a fucking loser for thinking that because that female is fucking smart and she'll see right through me. Should I send a text message too? No! Fuck, when did I grow a fucking vagina? I stare down at my phone, willing it to ring, and hear her voice laughing through the speaker, threats spewing from her mouth. Nothing.

Fuck it, I've clearly already lost my balls, what's the harm in one text? I send her a short text asking for a phone call when she gets the chance, like the little bitch I am, but when the phone stays silent, I throw it on the bed and stalk back out to the main room. Darius and Santos are still talking about what they'll do to punish Selene and I curse as my cock swells in my pants. She really does take those punishments like a fucking champ.

I lean against the wall, staring at the front door, and thinking about where Blaze might be right now and if he has any idea of where Selene is. How long before he's back with her thrown over his shoulder and cursing him? How long until she's back under me where she fucking belongs?

I've never felt like this before. My heart is twisting painfully as confusion takes hold.

Did she really leave us? I don't want to believe it, but something deep down tells me she's gone.

No one has ever matched my crazy, but Selene slots in perfectly beside me, not batting an eye at my openness in the bedroom with Darius. We've always messed around because it feels good, why would we deny ourselves of that?

She's fucking perfect, and I'm never letting her go.

Darius grabs the back of my neck firmly in his hand and tugs my face around to look him in the eye, his swimming with mixed emotions.

"Stop it. She didn't leave to hurt us, she did it for her sister. You heard Blaze," he murmurs in a low voice, trying to draw me out of my own emotions. If anyone could, it's him. He's been my anchor for so fucking long that I know I can't function properly without him now.

"Doesn't mean I'm not fucking hurting," I rasp out, letting him see my pain. He always sees me.

He rests his forehead on mine, knowing his closeness calms me down.

"I know, I hurt too. Blaze will bring her back, then we can get her between us and remind her who she belongs to."

I close my eyes and focus on my breathing, not wanting to get out of control. If I think about it for too long, I'll lose my fucking mind, then anyone within a ten mile radius of me is in trouble. I'll burn the town down to find her if I have to, and Darius knows it.

"What if he can't find her?" I finally ask, not surprised by his response.

"Then we set some fires and smoke her out. She's good at hiding, but we're good at finding. Between Blaze hunting her down and the people we know, someone will spot her at some point. Now, pull yourself together and box the crazy away. Let it out to play later if we need it," he orders, waiting for me to nod before he ruffles my hair and sits back.

For everyone's sake, I hope Blaze finds her because if he doesn't? I won't be able to keep my shit together for long.

Darius

Can't lie, I'm worried. Santos won't contain his emotions for more than a day or two, then we're all fucked. We won't be able to contain him once he goes on a rampage, and I hate to think of how much damage he'll cause.

I love seeing him mesh with his crazy when he's passionate about something, but usually it's just his excitement to cause blood and mayhem. His feelings for Selene are so strong, that I know he'll destroy himself without her.

"I'm going to punish her so bad when I get my hands around her throat," Santos confirms, nodding briskly as if agreeing with himself. His hands tighten on his lap as he thinks, his brow creasing in the process.

"I'll bend her over my lap and hold her still while you spank her," I reply, his eyes flashing to mine with a small grin.

"I'm going to do more than spank her. She won't be able to sit for a month once my dick leaves her tight body. I want her to choke on your dick so bad that she passes the fuck out."

"Don't you remember what happened the last time we tried that?

She head butted your junk and punched me in the guts," I snort, his eyes flashing almost cruelly.

"Can't swing at us if she's knocked the fuck out. If she can swing, you're not far enough down her throat," he chuckles, leaning back to rest his head on his arms. "I'll bind her wrists behind her back, just in case."

"Do you think she'll let us use blood as lube again? Fuck, my cock got so hard last time," I growl, my cock twitching in my pants.

"She'll damn well do as she's told or I'll gag her. Well, she'll be gagging on your cock any way so how can she complain?" he asks seriously.

He has a point.

Zander's glaring at the door, half paying attention to our conversation while deep in thought. Our fucking group dynamic has fallen to pieces from Selene tearing it down, and we are crumbling without her now.

She's become the air we breathe, and there is no other option but to bring her home. The pain will eventually turn into anger, and anger will fuel the fire inside of us until we explode and let chaos reign.

She has no idea what she's done by leaving us instead of bringing us along to help, but she'll sure as fuck find out when we catch up to her.

Epilogue

Selene

My phone pings with a message from Zander and I lock away the slight twinge of guilt with the rest of my feelings. I don't have time to miss them and I don't have enough space inside of me for feelings. I'm finally on the right path to my sister and those four men won't fuck this up, or else my pretty knife will be through their throats, and my bloody scythe on their foreheads.

I sink back into my seat and watch the New York City scenery pass me by through the bus window. I found a few entries in the ledger for the year my sister was taken that could match her description and both were sold to a MC gang in Nevada. I like the thought of heading into a large compound filled with big burly bikers and gunning it down for my sister. I will raze all of Nevada to the ground if it means I find her and I'll enjoy every fucking minute.

Can I find a blimp to fly over the state afterward with a large *Reaped* painted into the side?

The End

Acknowledgements

Hey Rach! Aren't you glad I forced you to write words on a shared Google doc? I'm glad I did because we did an amazing job and I got to find another author just as crazy as me! I love you and thank you for taking the chance! Let's do it again.

Since we smushed our Betas together for this one I need to go look up all the names. Samantha, Amber, Jocelyn, Gemma, Kristen, Tash, and Stephanie, thank you so much for delving into our baby, your help was so very appreciated.

To our editor Lori, yes you can have Santos, and yes we will write a continuation at some point. Thank you for all the enthusiasm and I hope you actually edited this, LOL.

Samantha and Lisa, we don't have much to say beyond what was in the dedication, but we clearly fucking love the hell out of you both and thank you for this opportunity.

To our readers both new and old, thank you for giving our story a shot, and thank you for supporting our new journey together. This one is about to get messy!

About the Authors

C.A. Rene

C.A. Rene is married (but dreams of a RH of her own) with two kids (assholes) and lives in beautiful (cold most of the year) Toronto, Canada. To escape from life's pressures (more assholes) she brings fingers to keyboard and taps out her imagination. Most of the stories floating in her head contain blood, angst, and dark dark love.

Lover of all things dark. I love to read it, write it, own it, eat it, whatever it. My addictions include WINE, books, and coffee, in that order.

R.E. Bond

R.E. Bond is a dark romance author from Tasmania, Australia. She is obsessed with reverse harem books, especially if they have M/M! She collects paperbacks as a hobby, has read or written every day since she started high school, and constantly needs music in her daily life. She loves camping and rodeos in the summer, and not getting out of bed in the winter. Coffee and books are life, and curse words are just sentence enhancers.

Also by R.E. Bond

Watch Me Burn

PRETTY LIES
TWISTED FATE
BEAUTIFUL DECEIT
IGNITE ME
PERFECTLY JADED

Reaped

THE REAPER INCARNATE

Also by C.A. Rene

Whitsborough Chronicles

THROUGH THE PAIN
INTO DARKNESS
FINDING THE LIGHT
TO REDEMPTION

Whitsborough Progenies

IVY'S VENOM
CARMELO'S MALICE
SAXON'S DISTORTION

Desecrated Duet

DESECRATED FLESH
DESECRATED ESSENCE

Hail Mary Duet

BLUE 42

Reaped

THE REAPER INCARNATE

Sacrificial Lambs

SING ME A SONG

Stay Connected

C.A. Rene

www.carenebooks.com

https://www.facebook.com/groups/carenereadergroup

words that drip blood and tears

R.E. Bond

www.rebondbooks.com

https://www.facebook.com/groups/prettypsychos

CPSIA information can be obtained
at www.ICGtesting.com
Printed in the USA
BVHW031830170722
642355BV00012B/508

9 781638 470564